Her head cleared the opening.

Blinded by the sunny light of day, she squinted, her even white teeth flashing with her wide smile. Light brown hair, almost blond, worn short and brushed back in a windblown style, framed the ivory skin of her face. She stood only a couple of inches over five feet and wore well-washed jeans with one of those comfortable floppy shirts.

Her mouth widened in surprise when her feet shot out from beneath her. She quickly came down the slide, landing solidly on the ground.

"How graceful," she murmured, her face reddening.

Eli offered his hand. "I'm sure it's easier when you're three feet tall."

Her laughter rippled through the air, her teal eyes closed slightly with merriment. *Probably in her early thirties,* he guessed, after spotting a few character lines.

Striking, Eli added to his earlier appraisal as he helped her to her feet. When her brows lifted and she pulled gently, he released her hand.

She dusted off the seat of her pants. "That was a masterful rescue. I didn't know how I was going to get Davey out of there."

"I'm thankful it worked," he said.

TERRY FOWLER makes her home in North Carolina where she works for the city of Wilmington. The second oldest of five children, she shares a home with her best friend who is also her sister. Besides writing, her interests include doing genealogical research through the Internet and serving her small church in various activities.

Books by Terry Fowler

HEARTSONG PRESENTS
HP298—A Sense of Belonging
HP346—Double Take
HP470—Carolina Pride
HP537—Close Enough to Perfect

Look to the Heart

Terry Fowler

Heartsong Presents

To my Aunt Inez, the woman with a heart big enough to share with all her nieces and nephews. Thanks for always being there for us.

A note from the Author:
I love to hear from my readers! You may correspond with me by writing:

Terry Fowler
Author Relations
PO Box 719
Uhrichsville, OH 44683

ISBN 1-59310-249-6

LOOK TO THE HEART

Our mission is to publish and distribute inspirational products offering exceptional value and biblical encouragement to the masses.

All scripture quotations are taken from the HOLY BIBLE, NEW INTERNATIONAL VERSION®. NIV®. Copyright © 1973, 1978, 1984 by International Bible Society. Used by permission of Zondervan. All rights reserved.

All of the characters and events in this book are fictitious. Any resemblance to actual persons, living or dead, or to actual events is purely coincidental.

PRINTED IN THE U.S.A.

Or check out our Web site at www.heartsongpresents.com

one

What had he gotten himself into now?

Eli McKay paused in the doorway, tightening his hold on his daughter. Lynnie had started to bounce excitedly in his arms on seeing the other children squealing and running around the day care center.

"Oh, excuse me!" the young woman behind him cried. His sudden stop had caused her to plow into his back.

He turned toward her and grinned. "I'm sorry. I'm not used to seeing so many kids at once."

Adults dotted the playground, their attention focused on the children. He watched as an older woman spoke to an active little boy then bent down and hugged him. Eight months of fatherhood had showed him one child could be a handful. He admired these people.

Minutes earlier he'd been waiting in the office of the day care center to fill out an application. The same young woman, a staff member named Gina, had come in to telephone a child's mother. Eli couldn't help but overhear when she asked for Janice Gore, only to find her away from her office. After he explained that he knew Janice and her son, Davey, Gina told him why she was calling Janice—Davey was holed up in a big pipe and wouldn't come out. Eli had offered to help.

Perhaps he'd been too quick to respond. But he owed Janice. After all, she had suggested the day care center to him.

"Come on, baby girl," he said to his daughter. "Let's see what our friend Davey's up to now."

The baby cooed as she took in the new sights and sounds. She patted her hand in his hair, and Eli prepared for the inevitable tug. She had a mighty grasp when it came to her daddy's hair. He'd be lucky if he had any left by the time she started walking.

Eli followed Gina over to what had to be the strangest playground equipment he'd ever seen. The large round plastic pipe stood on stilts, a bend dividing the ten or twelve feet before dropping off into a five-foot slide.

Somewhere in the bowels of the contraption, he could hear a woman chatting with a child—it had to be Davey—as though they were in a bright, cheery classroom.

"The bogeyman is in here, Ms. Dee," the small voice said. "Billy says he lives in the dark."

"Davey, there is no boogeyman. Billy's just trying to scare you."

"Mommy and Daddy stay with me when I'm afraid."

"Grab my hand," she said at his wavering response. "We won't be afraid of the dark any longer."

Soft and distinctly feminine, Eli found her words reassuring and intriguing. "Who's in there with him?" he asked Gina.

The young woman giggled. "Our fearless director. I hope she doesn't get stuck inside that pipe."

Eli chuckled and continued to eavesdrop, his imagination running wild as he visualized the female who told Davey she could eat a zillion chocolate chip cookies in one sitting. Not and fit in this tube she couldn't.

He jerked himself back to the emergency. "Davey? It's Mr. McKay. Come on out."

Lynnie bounced against his chest, babbling her own request.

"It's dark." The tiny voice sounded as if it were in the bottom of a drum.

"Must not be the Davey Gore I know," Eli said. "That Davey sleeps in his own room without a night-light. His mom thinks he's the bravest little guy in the world."

The child cleared the opening in a flash. "It's me, Mr. McKay."

Eli feigned shock. "Why, it is my Davey. Come on out, buddy." He reached out to help, but the child plunked down on the slide and raced to the bottom, landing on his feet.

Davey ran off to play, and Eli turned back to the apparatus, catching the woman's voice again, this time mumbling dire warnings about the monster's future existence.

"Owie! Oh! Owie!"

As the groans and grunts blended with what sounded suspiciously like giggles, Eli called, "Are you okay in there?"

"I'm—" the voice began, a groan taking over. "My toe— cramp."

Her head cleared the opening. Blinded by the sunny light of day, she squinted, her even white teeth flashing with her wide smile. Light brown hair, almost blond, worn short and brushed back in a windblown style, framed the ivory skin of her face. She stood only a couple of inches over five feet and wore well-washed jeans with one of those comfortable floppy shirts.

Her mouth widened in surprise when her feet shot out from beneath her. She quickly came down the slide, landing solidly on the ground.

"How graceful," she murmured, her face reddening.

Eli offered his hand. "I'm sure it's easier when you're three feet tall."

Her laughter rippled through the air, her teal eyes closed slightly with merriment. *Probably in her early thirties,* he guessed, after spotting a few character lines.

Striking, Eli added to his earlier appraisal as he helped her to her feet. When her brows lifted and she pulled gently, he released her hand.

She dusted off the seat of her pants. "That was a masterful rescue. I didn't know how I was going to get Davey out of there."

"I'm thankful it worked," he said. "His mother is an exhausted woman vowing to wreak havoc on the older child who introduced her son to the boogeyman."

The young woman heaved a sigh. "After this escapade I'd be almost tempted to give her his name."

Lynnie took that moment to dive forward, her arms outstretched. Eli reacted quickly, securing her in his hold. One of these times she was going to take a nosedive right out of his arms.

"And who is this little beauty?" she asked, tickling the baby's chin.

Lynnie hid her face in his shoulder. Eli smiled. "My daughter. We're here to discuss enrolling her in your center."

"Do you have a couple of minutes?" She glanced around the play area. "I need to make sure Davey's okay, and then we can go to the office."

"Sure. We can wait."

He watched her work her way across the playground and found himself thinking of the Pied Piper when several children trailed behind.

His attention was diverted to two boys who were chasing each other. He stepped back to give them room, his gaze drawn back to the director as she sank to her knees in the sandbox beside Davey.

Did he really want this for his daughter? Very much so. This woman obviously had a remarkable rapport with kids.

She caught Davey's hand, leading him back to where Eli waited. "Thanks again for helping," she said.

"I've known Davey far too long not to help. Janice works for me."

She nodded. "Welcome to Kids Unlimited. I'm Diedra Pierce." She reached to shake his hand.

"Eli McKay."

Davey fidgeted at her side, obviously unimpressed by the adult conversation. "Ms. Dee," he said, tugging impatiently at her shirt, "can I play?"

Her hand dropped away and came to rest on Davey's shoulder. "Thank Mr. McKay first."

The little boy mumbled the words then ran off to the swings.

"So much for undying gratitude," she said with a shrug.

"That's some playground equipment."

Her expression came alive with her grin. "A former enrollee's father created the tunnel slide. I should have refused, but he insisted. It's too dark in the tunnel."

"You could always install low-voltage strip lighting."

She smacked her forehead and groaned. "Why didn't I think of that?"

"Do they all call you Ms. Dee?"

She nodded. "It's easier for the kids. Why don't we go to the office?"

Diedra turned to go inside when the two boys ran ahead of her and collided. They fell in a jumble of arms and legs and pained cries. Diedra helped them up and checked to make certain they were okay. "Stop chasing each other," she instructed firmly. She glanced at Eli and shook her head. "It must be a full moon or something. Today has been one of *those* days."

Eli pulled open the door and waited for her to enter. "I imagine all your days are action-packed."

"Definitely," she agreed.

A huge contemporary desk and a credenza holding all sorts of computer equipment occupied one corner of the room. A cushy but worn navy leather couch sat against another wall, with a floor lamp next to it, and a small children's activity area filled the opposite corner. He sat in one of the two blue leather wingback chairs she indicated.

"Did Sarah give you an application?

Eli reached for the clipboard that rested on the chair arm. "I think I answered everything. I got sidetracked when your staff member came in."

Diedra settled in her desk chair. "So why are you considering day care?"

Eli pulled a toy from his coat pocket and handed it to his daughter. "I've run the gamut from babysitters to housekeepers to a nanny. My nanny just quit without notice to get married. Guess she figured she wouldn't need a referral. I'm desperate."

"I see."

From her tone he knew she'd misunderstood him. "What I mean is that I need people I can depend on to be there on a daily basis. I wouldn't be here if I didn't think day care would work for my child."

She nodded, and the room grew quiet as she studied the pages. No doubt his atrocious handwriting caused her difficulty. Even he had trouble reading the bold black slashes at times.

"Gerilyn?" She glanced up for confirmation.

"Actually it's pronounced Gerry-Lynn. It's a combination of my parents' names," he explained.

"Father—Elijah," she read aloud. "Gerilyn's mother is. . . Oh, I'm sorry."

Her gaze focused on him once more. He'd dreaded this

moment from the time he had written "deceased" in the space allotted to the mother's name.

Eli nodded at her sympathetic words. Even if questions filled her head, she didn't ask. He had to give her that. Diedra Pierce didn't allow curiosity to cross the boundary of professionalism.

"She's eight months old?"

Relieved she'd moved on, he nodded again.

"The problem is we don't have an opening for her age range," Diedra said.

"Surely you can make an exception. Janice raves about your center."

She shook her head. "I'm thankful our parents think highly of our day care, but state law prohibits overcrowded classrooms. We do maintain an application backlog. I'd be happy to put your daughter's name on the list."

Nothing seemed to be going right lately. "I suppose it's the only choice I have. What sort of time frame are we looking at?"

"We never know. Parents may withdraw their child today, or we might not have an opening for months. I can tell you we have one parent who is considering withdrawing her child. Gerilyn would be at the top of the list if that happened."

"I'd hoped to get this sorted out today."

"There are other centers," Diedra said.

"True, but yours comes with high recommendations."

"Recommendations are great, but we have to make sure Kids Unlimited is a good fit for your daughter."

He'd seen more love, warmth, and caring than he'd ever dreamed of finding for his child. "I already know your center will be a perfect fit. How many directors do you think would crawl into that tube to get to a child?"

Her cheeks colored.

"You did that because you cared about Davey," he continued. "You took care one extra step, and that's what I want. My daughter's happiness is my only goal."

"It's our goal, too."

Lynnie jumped in his lap, and Eli tightened his hold again and glanced down at her. Sometime in the past few minutes she'd managed to lose a shoe and sock. He straightened the tiny pink bow that circled a wisp of dark hair and smiled when she tried to stuff her toy into her mouth. He looked at Diedra. "Tell me about this backlog."

She leaned forward as she began to talk. "Basically I conduct an interview today. When a slot in her age group becomes available, I contact you. You get her physical form completed, and we enroll Gerilyn. Do you want to proceed?"

"Definitely."

Eli waited as she finished reading the application. The back of the chair cushioned his head, and he allowed his thoughts to drift to the work waiting for him. He'd spent a great portion of the past few days and nights sorting through designs for next year's furniture line. Those same hours included rescuing Lynnie from the things she'd managed to find during her crawling excursions.

Taking her to the office wasn't the solution. Now that she was more active, he couldn't keep up with her and work. He often placed her in the playpen and listened to her whine until she occupied herself with a toy or fell asleep. It made concentration nearly impossible.

Now she had her day and night hours confused and spent half the night wanting to play. Probably because he encouraged her to take longer naps during the day.

A nap didn't seem like such a bad idea right now. His eyelids were so heavy. He allowed them to close. Just for one second.

two

The baby's cry caught Diedra's attention, and she glanced up to find Eli McKay asleep and his daughter reaching for the toy she'd dropped on the floor. Diedra hurried around the desk and retrieved the plastic ring. The baby flashed a grin before hiding her face against her dad's chest. Diedra found her shyness adorable.

Eli jumped with the baby's movement, his eyes opening. "What happened?"

"She dropped her toy."

He swiped a hand over his face. "Sorry. I dozed off."

"I noticed. You want to continue this later?"

"I'm tired, but I don't know when I'd find time to come back."

The baby dragged her father's tie toward her mouth. He quickly diverted her attention and tucked it back inside his coat. Diedra's gaze rested on the delicate baby girl. The "I Love My Daddy" on her ruffled pink stretch suit said it all. "She resembles you."

He grinned. "Poor baby. She'd have done better to take after her mother."

"Oh, but she's a beautiful child."

Heat crept over Diedra's face. She might as well have told the man he was handsome. She did find him attractive, but it wasn't something she needed to point out to him.

"Lynnie and I thank you," he said with a smile and a nod of his head. "Thanks for coming to her rescue."

"Let's finish this so you can catch a nap." Diedra sat on the edge of the desk and reached for the clipboard and pencil. "Primarily we need to know a little about Gerilyn. Let's see. No allergies. Unique behavior characteristics? Eating? Sleeping?"

Eli answered, and she jotted the information on the page. She covered the entire questionnaire, asking and receiving clear, concise responses. Several times Diedra found her attention drawn to the bass textures of his voice.

Diedra reached for a brochure and went over the information listed there before passing it to him along with a form for a doctor's physical. Lynnie grabbed at the colorful paper, but Eli quickly tucked it away in his coat pocket.

"We use age-appropriate activities to stimulate the child's development. Is she this active all the time?"

"Yes. She's smart, but then I'm her father. What else do you expect me to say?"

"Why don't you leave her with us for a couple of hours? Go home and get a nap," Diedra suggested when he yawned widely. "Think of this afternoon as an experiment. See how she adapts."

"I don't suppose you have an extra cot tucked away somewhere? I didn't realize how tired I was until I sat in this chair."

Concerned, she asked, "Should you be driving?"

A wry smile touched his face. "Probably not."

"Use the couch over there," Diedra offered. "I can vouch for its comfort, but I can't promise peace and quiet. Not with children on the premises. Expect some laughter, loud talking, a little screaming, crying maybe. Then again, after the day we've had. . ."

"I'll take my chances. Though I doubt anything will wake me once I close my eyes."

"I'll put Gerilyn in the nursery." Diedra held out her arms, and the baby moved willingly into her hold.

"Lynnie," he said. "I call her Lynnie."

She nodded and walked out into the hallway. "You're a pretty girl," Diedra cooed to the baby as they headed down the hall.

The nursery was quiet with most of the babies sleeping. "I have a visitor for you," she told Gina. "Her dad is dead on his feet."

"Not bad to look at either, from what I saw," Gina said, smiling.

Diedra knew the direction this conversation would take. All the women in the center wanted her to have someone special in her life. A few of them had tried to set her up with blind dates, but she had managed to resist their plans. "Don't even think about matchmaking." They smiled, and Diedra slipped into the hallway.

She returned to the office to find Eli McKay fast asleep, his tie loosened, shoes off, looking comfortable all stretched out. Diedra looked at him for a few seconds longer. Why had she offered her couch? Perhaps because of the dark circles under his eyes or her suspicions that fatherhood proved more difficult than he'd expected—and then again probably because she wanted to help him in some way. His obvious disappointment at hearing they didn't have a slot open for his daughter bothered Diedra.

She studied him for several moments. Good looking in a rough sort of way, he wore his blond-streaked brown hair brushed straight back in a style that reminded Diedra of swashbucklers of old. His scraggly beard gave him the unkempt look an actor had made popular years before. He was long and lean, and the tailored suit fit him superbly, as did the white silk shirt.

Quit ogling him, she chastised herself, moving to her desk to focus on the food orders for the upcoming week. Diedra found herself struggling to justify the frequent glances in Eli's direction.

He slept restlessly, his frequent tossing and turning making the old couch creak and groan. Feeling the chill in the room, Diedra drew an afghan from the back of another chair and covered him. She fought the urge to sweep the hair from his eyes and decided it was time to find somewhere else to be.

"No!" His shout filled the room.

Diedra froze, her head telling her not to get involved, her heart saying it was too late. She knelt by the chair and found herself staring into his startling pale blue eyes.

"You didn't leave."

Confused by his statement, Diedra knew she should say something, but shock wedged the words in her throat. His eyes drifted closed, and she realized he'd been talking in his sleep.

Diedra studied his face. Warning flags shot up in her head. *Be sensible.* She couldn't be attracted to this man. She hurried from the room.

❧

The after-school children arrived, and Diedra busied herself with her tutoring duties. She fought the desire to check on Eli, to assure herself he rested comfortably. At the thought, apprehension gripped her. She returned to the task of explaining algebra to a young man.

At six o'clock Diedra said good night to the last of her staff. Gina hesitated at the front door, motioning toward Eli on the couch. "He's still asleep?"

Diedra nodded. "I should wake him."

"He must be exhausted. Want me to stick around for a while?"

Diedra considered Gina's offer. In all fairness she couldn't ask the woman to stay. "No. It's okay."

"Lynnie's in the baby swing. See you tomorrow."

"Thanks, Gina."

Diedra made her final daily walk-through of the ground-floor rooms in the old two-story Victorian house. She'd had the entire area reworked into functional classrooms. The primary goal of every activity area was accessibility to the children. Crayon and finger-painted artwork, bearing the names of the creators, covered every available inch of bright cheery walls.

As always, she thanked God for giving her this oasis of peace, for filling her life with so much love. Kids Unlimited was Diedra's commitment to the future. She and her staff were more than caretakers. They were more than teachers. They loved these children as if they were their own.

"Diedra? Are you there?"

At the sound of Janice Gore's voice, Diedra moved toward the side door. Surely it wasn't six thirty already. When Janice had mentioned her anniversary earlier in the week, Diedra had arranged for her to bring the children over for the night.

"Diedra?" Janice's voice grew louder.

She opened the French doors, and Davey shot past her, making car sounds as he sped his toy car through the air. Taking Janice's nine-month-old daughter, Kaylie, into her arms, Diedra kissed the baby's forehead and spoke to Janice. "I met your boss today. He rescued your son."

Janice groaned, looking around for Davey then finding him by the toy box. "Sarah told me when I picked them up earlier. Did Eli enroll Lynnie?"

"We discussed it. Nothing's been finalized."

"I was certain he'd enroll her. Eli's been frantic with trying to find a place for Lynnie and dealing with the business,"

Janice said. "He's been bringing her to work this week. From what he says, they're sitting up half the night. I hoped you'd be able to help."

"I'm sure we'll discuss it further. Once a slot becomes available."

Janice frowned. "I didn't think about that."

Lynnie's cries turned Diedra's gaze to the now idle swing. She walked across the room, with Janice behind her, and attempted to placate the baby with a pacifier.

"Why is Lynnie here?"

"Her dad's sleeping in my office."

Janice smiled. "So that's where Eli's been."

Davey raced by, shouting at the top of his lungs, and Diedra took advantage of the confusion to catch her breath. Janice's sigh made her laugh.

"Evidently he's over his earlier scare," his mother said. "I'm sorry that happened."

"Davey provides the excitement in my boring life," Diedra told her.

"Excitement?" Janice repeated. "Is that what you call it?"

Diedra grinned. "Well, some people might refer to Davey as a challenge."

"Definitely a challenge," Janis agreed. "I need to run. David's waiting in the car. He made reservations for eight o'clock. You have our cell number just in case?"

Diedra nodded. Strong longing filled her as she listened to Janice's plans for the evening. If her life were normal, maybe she'd be planning a romantic evening with her husband. Instead she was babysitting another woman's children so her friend could have time alone with her husband.

Don't think about this now, she told herself as she waved good-bye to Janice. Not that she had time to think. Juggling two babies and an active four-year-old tonight would keep her on her toes. While Lynnie played in the swing, Diedra gave Kaylie a bottle. Suddenly the silence struck her.

"Davey?" she called. What was he up to now?

Eli staggered into the room, the toy car in one hand and Davey's hand in the other. "Do you have any glue?"

"Davey, you shouldn't have awakened Mr. McKay. I'll take care of that," she said, reaching for the car.

"No. I want him." Davey hugged Eli's legs.

Eli smiled. "I can't resist four-year-olds who ask me to fix their broken cars."

Diedra went to the storage cabinets and located the glue.

Eli knelt in front of the swing then glanced at Diedra. "How's my girl doing?"

"She did fine. Slept on and off all afternoon then enjoyed being the center of attention."

"All afternoon?" He looked at his watch, his eyes widening. "Why didn't you wake me?"

"I figured you needed the rest."

"I guess I did," he agreed, running his hands over his bristly cheeks. "I'm starving."

"I need to fix something for Davey and me. Would you like to join us?"

"Thank you, but no," he said quickly. "I've taken advantage of your kindness too much already today."

"Leftover spaghetti and cheese bread," she said with a shrug. "Nothing fancy."

"No, really. I couldn't."

"One more won't make a difference," she said, overriding his protests.

"You make it difficult to refuse," Eli said. "What can I do to help?"

"Watch Davey and the girls."

He grinned. "Hmm. Maybe I should run out for burgers."

Diedra laughed. "I'll have supper ready by the time you glue that wheel back on."

Minutes later she had the meal on the table. She put a booster seat in one chair for Davey and pushed two high chairs to the table for the girls.

She walked into the nursery to call them to the table and paused to study the group on the play mats. Eli seemed right at home with the kids. Davey hung on to Eli's arm, and the two babies lay on the floor, kicking their legs in response to Davey's giggles.

"Dinner's ready."

Diedra picked up Kaylie, and Eli lifted Lynnie. Davey followed.

They settled around the table, Lynnie at her father's elbow, Kaylie at Diedra's, and Davey in the middle.

Eli kissed his daughter's forehead, and Diedra's heart skipped at the obvious show of love between father and child. She wished more kids had fathers like him.

Here's the well-rested Eli, Diedra thought as he settled into his chair. From what Janice had said, Eli had his hands full with both the business and Lynnie. With rest he had become charming and eager to please.

"Davey, would you like to say grace?" she asked.

"Mr. McKay can."

Eli asked a blessing on the food and started twirling spaghetti around his fork. Diedra almost laughed when Davey tried to mimic Eli's action.

They talked and laughed, and when Diedra led the conversation into casual topics, Eli responded. Davey quickly tired of the adult conversation, demanding their attention with his restlessness. Eli pulled him onto his lap and rubbed his whiskers against the boy's face.

Davey giggled. "You tickle."

Eli rubbed his hand over his face. "Guess I could use a shave. I thought a beard might be less trouble, but I'm not going to survive the growing-out period."

Diedra's attention veered to Davey, who was moving toward Kaylie's chair. "Don't you dare!" she said sharply.

Eli started. "What?"

"Not you." She glanced at Eli then jumped up to intercept the little boy. "Kaylie can't eat toast."

"But she's hungry. See—she wants it," Davey said, dangling the crust in his baby sister's face.

"Kaylie has to eat special food," Diedra explained, guiding Davey back to his seat. "I'll take care of her. Eat your spaghetti."

Diedra settled into her seat again and tried not to stare at Eli as he watched Davey. She enjoyed Eli's infectious laughter when the boy sucked down a strand of spaghetti and managed to get more sauce on his face than in his mouth.

"I never thought I'd enjoy kids so much," Eli told her. "Seeing Lynnie change on an almost daily basis has been wonderful."

"It's exciting," Diedra agreed. "It won't be long before she's walking and getting into everything."

"She's already getting into everything."

Kaylie's loud cry brought Diedra's attention back to her. She concentrated on soothing Kaylie, afraid the baby's agitation would set off a similar reaction in Lynnie.

"Janice told me Kaylie fights sleep," Eli said.

"She doesn't want to miss anything." Diedra rocked the baby in her arms.

"That must be Lynnie's problem, too."

They glanced over to where Davey played peekaboo with Lynnie. She hung over the side of the chair to look for him when he darted away, all smiles when he popped back up.

Eli stacked the dishes and carried them over to the sink.

"I'll take care of those," Diedra said.

"You cooked. I'll clean."

By the time he had finished, Kaylie had fallen asleep. "Looks as if she's down for the night," he said softly. He nodded toward Davey. "What time does he go to bed?"

"Eight thirty. After I put her down, I'll put him in the bathtub to wash off the spaghetti and read him a story before he goes to sleep."

"Come on, baby girl," he said, scooping up Lynnie from the high chair. "That's our cue to hit the road."

"I'm sorry I couldn't help you today. I'll call as soon as I know something for sure." She stood and followed him to the kitchen door.

"You helped more than you realize," Eli said. "I'll look forward to hearing from you."

She accepted his outstretched hand. "You're welcome to my couch anytime."

Eli squeezed her hand. "It was more than that," he said. Then he was gone.

❧

After putting the children to bed, Diedra curled up on the sofa. The television kept her company as she updated her financial records. She would never become a millionaire, but she had decided her well-being was more important. She'd dedicated her career to the children in her day care center. Besides her time with God, her time with them seemed to be the only right thing in her cockeyed world.

She shut off the laptop when the vision of Eli McKay appeared in her head. *Why does he intrigue me so?* Diedra wondered, frowning when the answer refused to present itself.

Suddenly the loneliness seemed overwhelming. Diedra reached for the phone but realized it was too late to call her friend Granny Marie. The older woman had probably turned in for the night around the same time as Davey.

She'd met Marie Wright the first Christmas after her grandparents died. Diedra carried on their tradition of visiting the nursing homes, and Marie had been more than happy to have a visitor.

They had grown close, and she had asked Diedra to call her Granny Marie as her grandchildren did. Granny Marie's unhappiness at losing her independence in the nursing home led Diedra to help. Now she came to the day care center during the day and went home to her son's at night.

Recently Granny had admitted feeling she was intruding on her son and his family. Diedra had given the matter a great deal of thought and prayer before inviting her to share the upstairs apartment. She knew the offer tempted her, but Granny feared she would hurt her son's feelings.

Diedra reached for the Bible on the end table and opened it to one of her favorite verses, John 14:27. "Peace I leave with you; my peace I give you. I do not give to you as the world gives. Do not let your hearts be troubled and do not be afraid," she read aloud, feeling grateful that her Comforter was always near.

"Lord," she whispered, "I come to You, seeking Your guidance in my walk with You. At times I feel like a newborn, uncertain how to proceed with the tasks You've set before me. I want to be the Christian You would have me be. I pray for strength to show love to those with whom You would have me share Your message.

"Support me in this task I've dedicated myself to. You know my weaknesses, and I pray You give me peace and understanding in the way You would have me go."

She whispered, "Amen," as Kaylie's cries began. She rocked the baby and wondered if Eli had gotten his daughter to sleep. She hoped so.

≈

Eli tried to move, fighting his way out of the darkness.

He opened his eyes to find the hour predawn, his stiffness the result of yet another night in his recliner. *The dream*, he thought.

Eli missed his wife. He remembered their last morning together as if it were yesterday, rather than nearly ten months before. Kelly was excited about traveling to Ohio to visit the young woman who had become an integral part of their lives. He'd kissed his wife good-bye and talked to her a couple of hours later when she called to tell him she'd arrived safely.

Sometime later he'd been doing his practice laps at the racetrack when they waved his car in. Kelly was dead. Another car had run a red light and struck her in the intersection. The police said she didn't see it coming. No doubt she was still excited. If only he'd been there with her. Perhaps she would have lived to see her dream fulfilled.

His gaze focused on the child sleeping peacefully in his arms. Kelly would have loved their baby girl. One thing was for certain: finding someone to care for her would not have been an issue if she were alive. His wife had wanted nothing more than to mother their child.

Eli glanced at the clock on the table. The brightly colored Kids Unlimited pamphlet caught his eye. Janice praised the center, raved in fact, assuring him he'd find no better in the city.

And with a child like Davey, Janice would know. Why ever would he want Lynnie enrolled at the same center as Hurricane Davey? He did, though—ever since he'd heard Diedra Pierce inside that tunnel.

Eli sighed. Why did things have to be this way? He prayed she would find a spot for Lynnie. She struck him as a loving woman. Efficient, attractive—someone he could like if he gave himself the opportunity.

But no matter how fascinating he found her, Eli knew he had a lot of healing to do before he could consider a relationship with any woman. Of course, that didn't preclude friendship.

"No one ever told us this was going to be easy, did they?" he whispered against his daughter's curls.

And if he were truthful, Eli would admit he didn't mind Diedra's attention. It seemed like a lifetime since he'd had a woman's interest, particularly one as loving and caring as Diedra Pierce appeared to be.

three

The feeling that she'd let Eli McKay down in his time of need weighed heavily on Diedra's mind. She tried to think of some way to assist him with child care, but beyond giving a few hours now and then, no solution seemed to work. Eli and Lynnie crept onto her prayer list, and she asked that God's will would be done in the situation.

And on Friday morning she received an answer to her prayers. One of the mothers decided to care for her six-month-old son at home. Diedra pulled the McKay application from the file and dialed his home number. "This is Diedra Pierce from Kids Unlimited."

She explained her reason for calling. "I wanted to let you know there's an opening. We can take Lynnie as soon as you get the form for her physical completed. I can give you a couple of days to make your decision."

"You have it now," Eli said without hesitation. "We'll see you on Monday at eight."

Diedra noted satisfaction in his tone. "I'll look forward to seeing you both."

The day passed quickly, and that night Diedra prepared dinner for Granny. She stirred a bubbling pot of green beans and prepared a tossed salad before checking the roast in the oven. "The nursery slot's filled. An eight-month-old girl named Gerilyn. She's so sweet. Absolutely beautiful."

"That didn't take long," Granny said, not missing a stitch as she rocked and knitted at the same time.

"It's just her and her dad. They came in the other day."

Diedra placed the salad bowl on the table before taking plates from the cabinet and rummaging in the silverware drawer. "Knowing Lynnie doesn't have a mom breaks my heart."

"You can't take all the children's losses to heart, Dee."

"I know what it's like not to have someone when you need them," she said, a faraway look glazing her eyes. The nightmare she'd lived with her husband before he died and her parents' failure to help haunted Diedra.

"Despite how you feel about them, you have a family, Diedra."

"They believed Benjamin's lies. They cared more about their precious name than they cared about me. I can't forgive them for that."

"They're only human."

Hearing Granny defend her parents hurt; Diedra was overwhelmed by the pain. Realizing Granny didn't know what had happened, she turned to her friend. "Benjamin killed my child and nearly killed me. They wanted me to drop the charges."

"Oh, honey, I'm so sorry," Granny said, dropping her knitting onto the seat and gathering Diedra in her arms. "Life dealt you a hard blow, but you know you'll have to forgive your parents—and Benjamin."

Diedra wiped her hand across her face. As always, the memories brought a flood of tears. Would she ever stop hurting? "How, Granny? How can I trust someone else when I can't trust myself?"

"You can trust God," Granny said. "You accepted Jesus Christ as your Savior and Lord, and that means you have faith that He will love and care for you. Faith equals trust. What if He sends the right man your way, and you shut him out because you don't believe He'll take care of your needs?"

"You can't understand what it was like for me," Diedra whispered.

Granny leaned back and looked at her. "No, I can't. For all of my seventy-seven years, I lived a sheltered life. I went from the home of loving parents to a man who treasured me, and now my son is dedicated to doing the same. I'm abundantly blessed.

"I'll never understand why your husband hurt you." Granny handed Diedra a tissue. "It's not your fault. To believe anything less is to give another undeserved victory to the same evil that allowed Benjamin to harm you. Why not give your fears to God?"

Diedra wiped her eyes. "I'm trying, Granny. God must be so disappointed in me."

"He isn't disappointed in you, dear. God loves and accepts you just the way you are. Don't forget that becoming a Christian is a growth process. We don't change overnight. It will get better."

Granny sat back in the rocker. Diedra washed her hands and returned to setting the table.

"What's Gerilyn's father like?"

She focused on telling Granny about the McKays rather than dealing with her own problems. "You should see him with his daughter," Diedra said, smiling. "He obviously loves her a great deal."

"So you like him?"

Everyone she knew seemed determined to see Diedra in a happy relationship. Even Granny looked at every man as marriage material. She wouldn't hesitate to play matchmaker if she thought she'd found the right man for Diedra.

"Not like that."

"Gina told me how handsome he is."

"I did my good deed for the day by letting him nap on my couch. And I'm committed to doing what I can to help them both," Diedra said, watching Granny's expression as she added, "the same commitment I give to all my parents."

Granny had told her more than once that she should stop giving so much of herself, but Diedra couldn't. Helping others made her feel her chosen path was worthwhile.

"Let's eat."

"I imagine Mr. McKay will be most appreciative of your help," Granny said as she took a seat at the table.

.

On Monday morning Eli stood in the doorway of her office, watching Diedra straighten the children's area. When he'd received her call, he'd been relieved to know Lynnie would be with people who cared. One person in particular—Diedra Pierce—stood out in his mind. He knew she would take good care of his daughter. And the idea didn't bother him at all.

But he feared his own fascination with Diedra. A fascination he couldn't afford. So many times since he and Kelly had decided to bring their child into the world, he'd questioned whether they'd done the right thing. But the moment he'd laid eyes on Lynnie, his daughter had grasped his heart in her tiny hand. He would do anything to protect her from harm.

.

Diedra tucked the stuffed animal in the basket and turned around. "Eli, come in." He held Lynnie in one arm and carried a huge bag stuffed with items in the other. Diedra doubted she'd ever seen one that large, even with the most protective of mothers. "Let me show you where she'll be."

Gina met them at the door. She greeted Lynnie and gave her time to warm up to her before taking her from her father's arms.

"I brought her favorite toys," Eli said. "Several bottles of formula, diapers, wipes—everything on the list you gave me. If she needs anything, call me."

Eli continued to talk, almost rambling, about the baby.

Diedra understood his separation anxiety. It would take a few days for both Eli and Lynnie to settle into the new routine. She touched his arm, and he paused.

"Feel free to check in often," Diedra said. "I doubt you'll find Kids Unlimited lacking. Did I tell you about our video monitoring?" He nodded. "Come into my office, and I'll give you instructions on how to check on Lynnie from your computer."

Eli kissed his daughter good-bye and walked to the door. He glanced back once more before following Diedra into the hallway. "You operate quite a business."

"I consider it more of a life mission. These children are important to us. They're our future, and we owe them a good start."

"Do you have a life outside this place?"

The personal question surprised her. "Not much of one," Diedra answered truthfully.

Silence engulfed them as they continued walking. A door opened, and an aide led a child out of a classroom and down the hall.

"I'd better get that information about the monitoring and head for my office," Eli said abruptly. "It'll be time to pick her up before I know it."

After he left, Diedra settled in her office and managed to get Eli off her mind long enough to focus on the lesson plans for the coming week.

≈

"Thanks, Diedra. I'll see you at eight thirty." He hung up the phone as Janice entered the office with two cups of coffee.

"Did you make your arrangements?" she asked. "David could have picked up Lynnie."

"He already has his hands full," Eli pointed out. "Diedra's keeping Lynnie until eight thirty."

Strange how contented he'd become in only one week. At

first he couldn't go through a day without checking on Lynnie. It hadn't taken long to realize how much the staff loved her. The staff and Diedra Pierce.

Diedra. Lately he'd taken to spending a few minutes in her office before collecting the baby. He loved hearing in her soft-spoken way how Lynnie had done that day. When she shared tidbits about her workday, he often did the same.

He smiled at Janice. "I've been meaning to thank you for referring me to the center."

"You'd better thank the Lord. She's the answer to my prayers, too."

"I have. Lynnie and I are particularly thankful."

"Diedra's a great person."

He picked up his cup and tilted back in his chair. "I didn't mean for her to take care of Lynnie tonight. I just asked her for a babysitter recommendation."

Janice sorted through the ring of fabric samples. "I think Diedra's a workaholic."

"She doesn't date?"

Janice shrugged. "It's a shame if she doesn't have someone in her life. Diedra suggested the kids stay overnight with her on our anniversary. She said we deserved adult time."

Workaholic. Eli understood that. McKay Design and Show-rooms had become his life after Kelly's death. He'd surrounded himself with the business, embracing the tasks with open arms, hoping to keep his mind occupied until he could fall into bed each night so exhausted he couldn't think.

"We'd better get through these, Eli," Janice said, pushing the fabric bundle at him. "Are you still thinking this shade of blue for the McNeils?"

&

Where has the time gone? Diedra wondered when the doorbell chimed. There never seemed to be enough for all the things she wanted to do. Grabbing a towel, she wiped her hands and hurried down the hallway. She could see Eli's image through the leaded glass panels of the front door, their beveled edges clouding his strong masculine profile. Maybe she should abandon her plan to invite him to dinner.

Diedra pulled the door open. "Hi. Come on in."

Eli stepped inside. "I'm sure you're busy. I'll just get Lynnie and go."

"Not really." She drew in a breath. "Have you eaten?"

He paused, his steady gaze boring into her. "I'll scramble some eggs later."

"Stay and have some chicken l'orange. I found the recipe in a magazine—main dishes in twenty minutes or less."

"No, really, I couldn't."

"You have to eat," Diedra reasoned. "There's plenty of food. I'm a fairly good cook. So if you don't stay, I'll think it's the company."

"Can't have you thinking that." Eli smiled. "Should I check on Lynnie?"

"If you want. She's asleep in the nursery. I have a monitor in the kitchen."

"It won't last. By midnight she'll be ready to rock the night out." Eli grimaced. "I can remember when rock had a completely different connotation. I'm praying these late-night play sessions end soon."

"Everything will be fine once she gets on a regular schedule," Diedra assured him, closing the front door.

Diedra could hardly believe she'd invited Eli to dinner. It hadn't been as difficult as she'd feared. For the first time in five years, she'd taken a step forward.

She enjoyed talking with Eli in the afternoons. A time or two she'd caught herself watching the clock, anticipating his arrival.

"You can wash up in the half bath under the stairs," she told Eli before he went to check on Lynnie.

"Anything I can do to help?" Eli asked when he came into the kitchen a few minutes later.

He'd removed his coat and tie and rolled up the sleeves of his pristine white shirt. Eli definitely rated a second look. And a third, Diedra allowed. "Everything's ready. How do you like your broccoli?"

"In the grocery store vegetable bin." He grinned.

"Now, Eli, we need our veggies," Diedra teased, stirring the cheese sauce before grabbing a pair of oven mitts. The silence caught her attention, and she turned toward him. Slight creases had formed in his cheeks, giving him a foreboding look. "Something wrong?"

He indicated the two plates and two glasses on the counter. "Did you plan this, Diedra?"

She couldn't deny she'd thought of him when she planned her evening meal. She disliked eating alone. Still, she hated feeling like a woman out to capture a man with her cooking. "If I say yes, will you accept it in the spirit intended?"

"Which is?"

Diedra opened the oven and lifted out the casserole dish. She placed it on a trivet and pulled off the oven mitts. "I admit to some selfish intent but with good motive. I wanted to cook. I knew you were coming and figured two friends could share a meal. Go ahead and sit down. I'll dish up the food."

"My social graces are obviously rusty," Eli muttered. The chair scraped across the wood floor as he pulled it away from the table.

Diedra filled two plates and placed one in front of him then sat down. "Nothing's wrong with your manners. Would you say grace?"

He bowed his head. "Heavenly Father, we thank You for

the food You've provided for us and ask that You use it for the nourishment of our bodies. Thank You for the loving care You provide us each and every day. In Jesus' name we pray. Amen."

"Amen," Diedra repeated.

He forked a portion of the mixture into his mouth and nodded approval. "Good."

"Thank you," Diedra said, offering him a napkin. "Hope you don't mind eating out of pots."

"Is there another way?"

She laughed. "Well, I have been known to allow my guests to serve themselves on occasion. Of course, this way is easier with the kids."

"You sound like Kelly. Kids were important to her, too."

"Kelly was your wife?"

Eli nodded.

"She must have been special."

Eli smiled. "The first thing she asked when I proposed was if we could have a dozen kids."

"And did you agree?"

"I suggested we have half that many. I had no idea then that children could be so rewarding."

He had touched on her favorite subject. "Yes, they are, and they're so challenging and full of love and inspire the strongest emotions. And they respect you when they know who's in charge."

"And here they know." Eli smiled again. "Your day care seems to be one of the most innovative around. How did you come up with the programs?"

Diedra took a sip of tea from her glass. "They revolve around two groups of people with pretty basic needs. We can fill their stomachs and keep them comfortable, but everyone needs someone who cares. Kids Unlimited cares."

"And Diedra Pierce. Why do you care so much?"

"For me, Mark 9:37 says it perfectly: 'Whoever welcomes one of these little children in my name welcomes me; and whoever welcomes me does not welcome me but the one who sent me.' I want people around me who care. There are never enough."

"That is certainly true," Eli agreed, a smile spreading across his face.

The way he looked at her made Diedra pretend renewed interest in the food on her plate. "Tell me about your work."

"What's to say about furniture design and sales?"

"You have to be kidding. It's one of the hottest things going in High Point," Diedra said. "I've read about the Southern Furniture Market. I'd love to go, but I know it's open only to members of the trade. I read that buyers come from every state and several foreign nations."

"We have another market coming up soon, but I'm not ready for it yet. In fact, I'm not sure I'll ever catch up on my work."

"I never seem to either," Diedra said. "But then if I did, I suppose I wouldn't have a job. Would you like seconds?"

"No, thanks. You're a good cook, though."

Diedra thanked him. "I have some great cookies if you'd care for dessert." She stepped over to the counter then returned with a half-dozen white chocolate macadamia cookies on a plate.

Eli sampled one. "Hmm. My favorite. Did you make them?"

"Granny Marie is my cookie baker. I'm sure you've met her. She helps out in the nursery."

Eli nodded. "So the kids get homemade cookies all the time?"

"Not always. We serve healthy snacks, too."

Eli ate the remainder of the cookie. "So tell me more about Diedra Pierce."

"I like helping others."

She thought back to the time five years earlier when she had showed up on her grandparents' doorstep in North Carolina. They shared their faith in God with her and did everything in their power to help Diedra realize her own self-worth.

She knew she had to put the past behind her, but it took time for a heart to heal. Hers still had a few rough edges. Forgiving and forgetting took time. Pain had a way of renewing itself when she thought of the past and all she'd lost.

Eli leaned back in the chair. "What else?"

"There's not much to tell. I have a master's degree in early childhood education. I'm a widow," she added, barely managing to get the words past the lump in her throat.

"I'm sorry. Recent?"

She shook her head. "A couple of years."

"What about other family? Parents? Siblings?"

"Only child. My parents live in California. Your turn."

Eli sipped his tea and returned the glass to the table. "You know I'm a widower, too. My parents died when I was twenty. My mom had cancer, and I suspect my dad died of a broken heart. I was an only child, too. They were older when I was born. I wish they'd had a chance to know their granddaughter."

"Perhaps they're smiling down on her from heaven."

"Are you a believer?"

She nodded.

"I came to know the Lord just a few months ago."

"Where do you attend church?" Diedra asked.

"Cornerstone. My parents went there. I attended as a child, but other pursuits became more important than serving the Lord."

"That's a huge church. I attend First Church. It was my grandparents' church."

"It's good having a church home."

"And a church family," Diedra added.

"I've met lots of good people in the last few months. Including those here at the center. I've been meaning to tell you I like the center's name."

"My grandmother suggested it," Diedra said, reaching for his plate. Eli moved to help, and she pulled back when their hands touched.

Diedra noted the way Eli hesitated, his speculative look, and found it impossible not to return his disarming smile. "My granny said she hoped I'd have so many kids these old walls would groan with the pleasure of their presence." Diedra paused. "Would you like coffee?"

Eli reached for the bread basket. "I'll help with these and then clear out so you can have a few minutes to yourself."

"I have a lot of those, Eli. This place is like a tomb when everyone leaves."

She reached for the coffee can on the top shelf. Too late, Diedra felt her shirt raise just enough for the ugly scar to show itself.

She glanced sideways and saw Eli staring at her arm.

"That must have been painful," he said.

She couldn't hide the scars forever, at least not that one.

Diedra jumped, and the coffee can slipped from her fingers, coming to rest on the edge of the countertop. Grounds flowed to the floor in a steady stream.

Eli reached past her to set the can upright.

She jerked her sleeve down. "It's nothing." Diedra refused to look at him. "I'll get the broom."

"Let me," he insisted.

The only sounds in the kitchen were those of dishes being washed, the swish of the broom, and, after Diedra summoned the energy to make coffee, the dripping of water into the pot.

Why hadn't she told him the truth about the scars? *Because you can't,* a little voice cautioned. *He'll lose respect for you.* Oh, why had she invited him to dinner in the first place?

Eli emptied the dustpan into the trash and replaced the items in the broom closet. "What's wrong, Diedra?"

"Nothing."

"I don't believe that, Diedra. You were fine until"—Eli broke off, resting his hand lightly on her arm when she tried to walk away—"I mentioned the scar."

Warning lights flashed in her head as Diedra stared down at his fingers. They seemed to tighten around her arm, and she became frantic, her skin paling and her breath coming in short gasps.

"Let go!" she demanded, jerking her arm away. "Take your hand off me. You have no right."

Eli dropped his hand at the terse request. As if on cue, Lynnie began to cry. Diedra could see him warring between his child's needs and wanting to understand what had just happened.

Tears squeezed from the corners of her eyes as she turned away from him. "You should take her home. It's past her bedtime."

"Diedra?"

"Just go, Eli. Please."

"Okay. We'll go. I'm sorry."

four

Diedra glanced at the clock for the tenth time in a minute. Her stomach churned with apprehension. They were late. He wasn't bringing Lynnie back.

Why should he? Diedra knew she'd frightened him with her behavior. She'd frightened herself as well. She could only attribute her reaction to fear. Fear she'd be hurt again. Fear someone else would let her down.

But that naive young woman her husband had tried to destroy no longer existed. And given a few years in this environment in which God had placed her, surrounded by children and good friends, she would get past the nightmare that had been her life.

Maybe it would be better if Eli didn't come back. If she didn't see him, didn't experience the pull of his charm every time they were together, perhaps she could avoid letting him overwhelm her life.

The front door opened. Eli stuck his head in the office, and Diedra's breath whooshed out.

"We overslept."

She moved to take Lynnie from him. Gently pulling the pink knit hat off her head, Diedra smoothed the fine hair back in place. "Another bad night?"

Eli frowned. "I couldn't sleep. I kept thinking about last night. What happened?"

Diedra looked at him. "It's not you. Maybe one day I'll be able to explain what happened. Right now I'm not sure myself."

"Enough said."

He smiled, and Diedra's smile blossomed from within. "I'll take her to the nursery if you're in a hurry."

"That would help tremendously. Bye, baby girl," he said, touching Lynnie's cheek with his finger. "See you both later," he added.

☙

Eli waited for the light to change then pulled into the line of traffic. Things had gone better than he hoped. In the early hours of the morning, he'd worried that he'd done irreparable harm to their strange friendship-working relationship. He'd startled Diedra by touching her arm like that. And by being nosy. He had no business interfering in her life. When it came to emotional baggage, he had a full freight car of his own.

As for pursuing a relationship with Diedra, it was too soon. Kelly hadn't been dead a year. He had to deal with his grief before getting involved with anyone. For now, his priorities were God, Lynnie, and the business.

Diedra's role as child care provider to his daughter had to be of prime importance. Of course, that didn't mean they couldn't be friends. Eli believed the more he learned about the women influencing his daughter's life, the more comfortable he would feel. Whatever the case, there could be no repeats of last night. The warm, almost datelike atmosphere of the evening had made thinking about the future seem almost too easy.

☙

Diedra ran into Granny Marie coming out of the nursery on Friday morning. "Well, hello, stranger."

"I could say the same."

"Come and visit me in the office when you get a chance," Diedra suggested.

A couple of hours later she sat in a chair next to the older woman. "So how are things with your family?" Diedra asked. "Any better?"

"Everything's rolling along just as Jimmy wants it."

Diedra noted Granny's irritation. She understood the woman's frustrations about growing old. Granny spoke freely of the curses, fragile bones, and declining health while her mental capacity remained undiminished.

Things had changed dramatically for Granny since her accident. She'd moved in with her son and his family and tolerated living in another woman's home—a difficult task for a woman who had run her own home for so many years.

"They're trying to make an invalid of me," Granny complained. "Jimmy hovers over me as if he's afraid I'll shatter. I'm surprised he hasn't wrapped me in cotton batting."

"He loves you."

Granny dropped her hands into her lap. "I know he does, but he's talking about selling my house and moving me in with him permanently. What kind of life is that? Francie and I are already driving each other crazy. Jimmy's focused on me like a germ under a microscope." Granny frowned. "He'd stay by my side day and night if I'd let him."

"He'll settle down eventually," Diedra said.

"Let's hope so. I can't stand much more of this. I wanted to bake a cake for Sunday dinner, and Francie started talking about how we didn't need the extra fat and calories. You'd think one little slice would kill her."

"She seems conscientious about her diet."

"Too much so. Jimmy and the kids shouldn't suffer because she gains weight by just looking at food. I miss my kitchen." Granny sighed.

"Feel free to use mine anytime," Diedra offered. "Go on a baking frenzy. These kids go through a lot of cookies."

"Not only the kids," Granny teased.

Diedra smiled. "Okay, so I can be bought with a handful of your Double Chocolate Delights."

The older woman laughed. "I'll remember that. I miss having people enjoy my cooking. Francie assesses every dish I prepare as if she can feel the fat corroding her arteries."

"Now, Granny, eating healthy isn't a bad thing."

"I don't want to interfere with her home, but I refuse to be treated like a child."

"You're always welcome here."

Regret filled her friend's expression. "I know. I just wish I could convince Jimmy to let go."

Diedra laid a hand on Granny's shoulder. "He will. Just give him time to get comfortable."

"Jimmy's just like his dad. He thinks everything is fine and dandy as long as the peace is maintained."

"Well, you know how to regain control of your life."

"Blessed is the peacemaker," Granny said.

Diedra shrugged. "It's a two-way street. Sometimes you have to fight for your own peace of mind."

"Honey, I have to remind myself it's in God's hands. He'll show me the way to go."

&

"You're lost in thought," Janice told Eli that afternoon when she stepped into his office.

"It's been a busy week."

"That it has. Any plans for the weekend?"

"Not really."

"Too bad. I imagine Diedra doesn't have any plans either."

He ignored her obvious hint. "I wouldn't know."

"But you could find out easily enough," Janice prompted.

"Why are you interested in my plans or hers?" he asked curiously.

"I think you two would make a nice couple."

Eli shook his head. "I'm not ready to be part of a couple. It's too soon."

Janice settled in his visitor chair. "But you like her, don't you?"

"It's too soon."

"Kelly wouldn't want you to grieve your life away. Not when you have a chance at happiness."

"You didn't even know Kelly," he countered, saddened by the fact that so many of his new friends never knew what a wonderful, supportive woman his wife had been. In fact, he'd noticed Diedra shared some of her traits. Kelly would appreciate the fact that Diedra was taking such wonderful care of Lynnie.

"I know Kelly loved you and you loved her," Janice said. "I know that when a woman loves a man, she wants him to be happy. You were blessed with a good wife."

"I was. And God took her away when Lynnie and I needed her the most."

"God works in mysterious ways, Eli. Don't close your mind if He sends someone to replace her. Grieve for her and move on. You deserve to find love again."

"I don't have time to invest in developing a new relationship."

Janice laughed. "Falling in love isn't something you schedule on your calendar. Once that feeling comes into your heart, nothing else seems as important. You find ways to be together even when you both have too much to do. You make time for everything else, don't you?"

"We'll see," Eli said brusquely, hoping to put an end to the conversation.

"Yes, we will," Janice said. "Just remember your heart has a mind of its own."

Janice's words confirmed the thoughts that had seemed to consume him. He missed Kelly. He missed being half of a couple. Kelly had been his sounding board and his confidante.

"Go home to David. I get the message."

"Sounds like a plan to me."

She started for the door, humming something that sounded like "Love Is in the Air."

"Very funny," he called to her.

If only falling in love this time could be as easy as the first. He'd felt this drawn to only one other woman. He'd found Kelly irresistible from the moment they met as seniors in high school. She listened to him dream about one day racing formula cars, and it became her dream, too.

They'd just celebrated their tenth anniversary the year she died. They'd been there for each other when their respective parents died and during the loss of their babies. They'd even come to know the Lord together. But they'd never had time to settle into a home life. And Kelly hadn't lived to mother the child she wanted so badly. How could he expect any woman to understand the decision he and Kelly had made?

Eli sighed. He didn't have time for this now. Besides, he didn't have a clue if Diedra felt the same. As always when his mind was troubled, Eli bowed his head and sought God's help in prayer.

❧

That afternoon Diedra worked in the kitchen, preparing for the fall festival at church later in the evening. She had signed up to bring candied and caramel apples. She stirred the caramel and reached for one of the apples.

Diedra could hardly believe October was nearly gone. The year had rushed away with alarming speed. Before she knew it, Thanksgiving and Christmas would arrive. She wouldn't think of that now. She had a lot to finish before she left for church.

❧

Pushing the kitchen door open, Eli watched Diedra pursue her task with the single-mindedness he'd come to expect. "Hello, Dee."

A soft scream accompanied her jump of surprise. She grabbed the apple out of the caramel coating. "Eli? What time is it?"

"A little after four."

"You're early."

He walked across the kitchen and settled on a stool. "I gave myself an early day. I was thinking I owe you a meal. Want to join Lynnie and me for dinner?"

"I can't." She gave the apple one last twirl and set it on the wax paper. "We have our fall festival at church tonight. Didn't you get a flyer?"

"I didn't read it."

"Several parents have said they'll bring their kids. I'm working at one of the games. Why don't you come, Eli? It'll be fun."

Granny pushed open the swinging door. "Eli, when did you get here?"

"A few minutes ago. Dee just invited me to the fall festival at her church."

"You're coming, I hope."

"I think we will."

"Good," Granny said, smiling broadly. "I'm heading for home. I need to pick up the cookies. See you later, Eli."

"Nice woman," Eli commented when Granny disappeared as quickly as she'd come. "Does she attend your church?"

"Sometimes." Diedra wrapped the candied apples in some cellophane.

"Want to ride with me and Lynnie tonight?"

"If you think there's room for everything I have to take."

"We'll manage," he said with a wink. "Need some help with those?"

"Two pairs of hands always get the job done faster."

five

"Looks like a good turnout," Eli said as he drove through the crowded lot a second time hunting for a parking space.

When she was appointed coordinator, Diedra and her committee had planned for the fall festival to be part of the church's homecoming celebration. They made a long list of activities that included games, prizes, food, a cakewalk, clowns, bobbing for apples, and a hayride in a horse-drawn wagon.

The committee posted notices around the city. Diedra sent public service announcements to the radio and television stations, and she'd seen to it that every Kids Unlimited parent received a flyer. A number had said they would see her at the church, but she knew to expect only a few.

Inside they'd decorated the large fellowship hall with the bounty of fall—pumpkins, bales of hay, colorful fall leaves, and scarecrows.

Eli looked around and nodded. "It looks good."

"Everyone pitched in to help," Diedra said. "I need to bring in the apples and drop off these prizes. I have the balloon board tonight. I can watch Lynnie if you'd like to explore."

"What's a balloon board?"

"The players attempt to burst balloons with darts as the board spins. They get tickets they can trade in on prizes at the end of the night."

"Sounds like fun. You're sure watching Lynnie will be no problem?"

She sat down on a nearby bale of hay and removed Lynnie's jacket. "Go have some of that fun I promised. We'll catch up with you later."

"I'll bring the apples in. Where should I put them?"

Diedra pointed to the table then took Lynnie with her to the area where they had set up her game. Occasionally Diedra caught glimpses of Eli in the crowd, talking with people or playing games. She propped Lynnie on her hip, and together they spun the wheel, staying well out of the range of the flying darts. When someone made a hit, Diedra gave tickets to the winner then replaced the balloons.

"You should have a few of those," a fellow church member commented when Diedra tickled Lynnie and made her laugh out loud. "You're a natural."

Diedra thanked her, choking back the fiery pain that welled in her throat. Had it only been five years ago the doctor told her she could never have children? The memory of it hurt as much now as his words did then.

When they were dating, Diedra never would have believed Benjamin capable of hurting her. In the end he'd deprived her not only of love but also of her dream of children. The old familiar lump closed her throat, and tears stung her eyes. Would the time ever come when she wouldn't hurt? When she wouldn't feel so empty?

Granny had walked up in time to hear the woman's comment. Diedra smiled faintly when her friend slipped an arm around her waist and hugged her. At times Diedra hated herself for the self-pity. If only she'd known about her husband's emotional problems. Perhaps her life would be different.

"Why don't you take a break? Find that handsome man who brought you," Granny said. "I'm pretty sure I can handle this thing."

Diedra smiled. "Thanks, Granny. Lynnie and I could do with a bit of liquid refreshment."

"Take your time." She turned to the line of people and smiled. "Okay—who's next?"

Diedra grinned when Granny expertly touted the merits of the spinning balloon board. Then she spotted Eli serving the kids and talking and laughing as he passed out cookies and candy. When one of the toddlers snatched another one's cookie, Diedra laughed at Eli's startled reaction. He immediately offered a replacement to the brokenhearted child.

She made her way to his side. "Having fun?"

He tousled the child's hair and stood. "Yes. I'm glad you nagged me into coming."

"Nagged?" She laughed. "You jumped at the opportunity. Did you bring a bottle? I think Lynnie's hungry."

"I had the ladies stash them in the fridge. I'll get one."

"Stay where you are. I need to get something to eat anyway."

In the kitchen, members of the refreshment committee surrounded Diedra. They warmed the bottle and cooed to the baby, all the while asking about Lynnie and her handsome father.

"You should snap him up," one lady suggested.

"We're friends," Diedra said.

The women looked at each other. "I wouldn't let him get away. No reason you should be alone when he's available and so needy."

Diedra had never considered Eli as anything but self-sufficient. Definitely not needy. What did it matter anyway? Even if he were, she couldn't be what Eli needed. *Don't think about him,* she told herself, knowing she would only become more depressed.

"I'd better feed her." Diedra tried to juggle the baby, a hot dog, and a cold drink. She smiled gratefully at the woman who carried the items out for her.

Eli came over to her then. "Let me take her so you can eat."

Father and daughter seemed lost in their own world as the baby lay in his arms, drinking her formula and playing with his face.

Diedra pushed her plate away. "Guess I'm not as hungry as I thought." She took a couple of sips of soft drink. Lost in her melancholy, she fell silent.

"Are you okay?" Eli asked, concern filling his voice.

She nodded, refusing to admit the turmoil inside her.

The baby drained her bottle and fell asleep across her father's lap. Eli made Lynnie comfortable and took Diedra's hand in his. "Want to talk?"

His caring gesture made her feel like crying. She shook her head and changed the subject. "I'm tired but happy the event is so well attended. Our homecoming is Sunday. You should come. We have dinner in the fellowship hall after church services. We have some great cooks."

"I've never eaten church food I didn't like."

"Me neither," Diedra agreed. She picked up her trash and rose to her feet. "I'd better relieve Granny."

Diedra was glad when the evening began to wind down. Kids agonized over how to spend the coupons they'd won while parents prompted them to hurry. Several children from the center came by to tell her good-bye.

"So what did you think?" Diedra asked Eli as he drove her home.

"I enjoyed myself. Several members invited me to come again."

"They're a friendly bunch," Diedra said. "They've been a blessing to me. I missed my grandparents so much, and everyone helped me through that period of my life."

"Losing loved ones is difficult," Eli agreed. "I don't understand why it has to happen. Kelly was so young. She had so much to live for."

As he spoke the words, Diedra considered her losses and the times she'd questioned God. A few tears of self-pity trailed down her cheeks; she welcomed the darkness. She hated these uncontrollable bouts of emotion.

In the backseat Lynnie whimpered.

Diedra looked back at the baby. "She's tired."

"Not Lynnie," Eli said, looking at his daughter in the mirror. "She's a real night owl."

"I thought she'd be sleeping the night away by now."

"I wish. Are you okay?" Eli asked. "You don't sound like yourself."

"I'm fine."

"Are you crying?" he asked, glancing at her.

"I'm okay," she murmured, turning her head to the window as she swiped at the remaining traces of tears.

"What happened?"

Diedra closed up at his question. Why couldn't she ever admit she'd been a battered wife? Because she felt shame about allowing it to happen? Because she hadn't been smart enough to stop Benjamin?

No matter how she tried to justify her behavior, she couldn't. She'd allowed Benjamin to use her for battering practice, to degrade and hurt her. As a result, she'd lost more than she cared to think about.

"Everyone gets the blues," she told him.

If only she could tell him why. But spousal abuse wasn't something one shared casually. Most of the time she presented a bright facade to the world and managed admirably, except for times like now when depression overwhelmed her.

"I'm sure even you have your moments," she said as he parked in the driveway. "Would you like to come inside?"

"I'll listen, you know."

Eli removed Lynnie from her car seat and attempted to calm the baby as they walked toward the house. The porch lamp cast a glow over his face, and Diedra saw Eli's sincerity.

It wasn't that she didn't want his help. Just not right now. His caring words had a powerful effect on her, and those silver-blue eyes touched her with the delicate probe of searching fingers. "It's nothing. Really."

Lynnie's continued crying took their attention from Diedra's problem. Diedra laid her hand on Lynnie's forehead and found it warm. She groaned. No matter how hard they tried, communicable diseases were a pitfall of day care. "Oh, Eli, I hate—"

"What?" He looked at her. "Diedra, tell me what's wrong with Lynnie. She's been crying for almost an hour. I don't know what to do."

"Calm down," Diedra said quietly, touching his arm. "We'll work on bringing her fever down, and if she doesn't get better, you should call her pediatrician."

"What?" The shouted word startled the baby into complete wakefulness, and her cries began in earnest. "Shush, honey. Daddy's sorry. Don't cry," he begged, rocking her gently.

Diedra's heart melted at Eli's frantic look. "Give her to me."

"How could this happen?" he asked, his voice rising again.

"You might as well prepare yourself," Diedra said. "As long as she's in day care, Lynnie will be exposed to everything."

He looked incredulous. "Don't you quarantine the sick kids? Send them home or something?"

"We try."

As Lynnie continued to cry, Eli moved closer to Diedra, her back blanketed by his chest as he reached over her shoulder to soothe his daughter. "Sweetie, please don't cry. Daddy's sorry you don't feel well."

Diedra found herself transfixed by the hand that consoled Lynnie. The gentle touch applied with just the right amount of control. His words were soft against her ear. "What can I do for her?"

"Come upstairs, and we'll see what we can do," Diedra said.

Eli followed so closely he bumped into Diedra when she stopped. Instinctively his arms cradled both her and his child. She stepped away quickly.

Upstairs in her sitting room, Diedra placed the baby on the sofa.

Eli paced the length of the small room.

"Eli, take it easy." Diedra reached up and pulled him down beside her.

She watched his hand go over his face in the gesture she'd begun to associate with him. "All it takes is exposure. The rest comes naturally. We are particular about sick children, but we can't spot everything."

He stood and paced again. "I know. I'm sorry. It's just that—"

"You hate to see her sick," Diedra finished for him.

He shoved his hands into the pockets of his slacks. "What should I do?"

"Let's sponge her off," Diedra said, trying to ignore the emotions swirling inside her. "Did you bring her bag in? We need to see if we can get her to eat."

He tapped his forehead. "I forgot her bottles at church. I'd hoped the car ride would lull her to sleep."

Diedra smiled. "Car trips worked in the past?"

He nodded. "Pitiful, isn't it?"

"Lots of parents, both mothers and fathers, use the same method," Diedra told him. "Look in the upper right-hand cabinet in the kitchen. We keep extra formula there. You should find a sterilized bottle as well. I'm going to put her in a cool bath."

Eli returned with a bottle of liquid medication. "I found this in her diaper bag." He disappeared again.

Diedra considered his reaction to Lynnie's illness. She'd never met a man with Eli's qualities.

"Hey, I can't find—" Eli entered the room and stopped, gazing at the scene before him. "How did you manage that?"

The crying had ceased. Lynnie lay there quietly, grasping Diedra's finger in her tiny hand.

"Lynnie loves the movement of the cradle swing. We have one in the nursery, too."

Fifteen minutes later they sat on the sofa, sipping the soft drinks Eli had poured in yet another kitchen run. Lynnie's eyes drifted open and closed with the sway of the cradle.

❧

Eli's gaze settled first on Diedra then on his baby in the cradle. "I have to ask you, Diedra. What have you done to my daughter? You know she cries when we leave the center."

Diedra looked up and smiled. "She's a discriminating baby."

His half smile changed to an expression of concern. "I worry that she's becoming too attached to you and the others."

"Lynnie will bond with the people who care for her, but I doubt she's crying because you take her away. More likely she knows she's in sympathetic arms."

"Are you saying she's spoiled?" The warmth of his smile permeated his voice as he looked at his child. "I love her so much."

A smile touched Diedra's lips. She stifled a yawn and murmured an apology.

"You're tired. I shouldn't have—"

"Nonsense," she interrupted. "I'm glad to help."

"Looks as if I'm going to get another break. I've just found the top of my desk in a couple of places. Oh well, no one ever said parenting was easy."

"No, but then everyone doesn't have access to Kids Unlimited's multifaceted plan. You work, and I arrange to go to your home until she's well enough to return to the center."

"You don't offer a program like that," he said. "Do you?"

"Well, no," she admitted, "but I think it would be a good idea if I could figure out the technical stuff."

Eli frowned and shook his head. "Probably not. Parents need to accept some responsibility for their children, you know."

"I can still help with Lynnie."

The idea tempted Eli. Letting Diedra take over Lynnie's care at the house would be too easy. While putting ice in the glasses earlier, Eli found himself thinking of the woman with his child. He shouldn't have stuck her with his problems. Her job demanded so much of her, days filled with kids, parents, and senior citizens. She didn't need to babysit a panicked father in the evenings.

But she wouldn't tell him that. She'd willingly do everything she could for him and Lynnie. He'd noticed that about Diedra Pierce. Along with her sharp mind, caring heart, beauty, and the other things that added up to make her a unique individual. She gave so much love to those around her.

"No," he said firmly.

"But—"

"You give too much," Eli said. "I could take advantage and let you come every day, but who's going to do your work here? I won't make more work for you."

Diedra flushed, and Eli knew he had hit on the truth of the matter.

"I care about her, Eli."

"And we care about you. I'll find a way. Now tell me why you were upset earlier."

Again he watched her close herself off from him. What was she hiding?

"Just one of those things. I let myself slip into the past and realized I'd made a mistake."

"I'll listen if you want."

"I think Lynnie's dropped off to sleep."

His gaze rested on the baby for a moment before coming back to her. "Thanks for putting up with us," he whispered, his arm dropping around her shoulders and squeezing her closer. "You're a lifesaver. I honestly don't know how we would manage without you."

"You'd do fine."

"I'm not so sure."

Eli wrapped her in a comforting hug, marveling at his attraction to Diedra. Her head rested against his chest. They both sighed at Lynnie's cry of protest when the cradle swing came to a gentle halt.

"I'd better get her home," he said. "Tomorrow's another long day."

"Not so long. Saturday sessions," she reminded him. "If you need to work, I can see if Granny's available."

"I have the weekend off," he said.

"You should monitor her temperature. If it rises again, contact her pediatrician. And feel free to call if you need me."

"I will."

As they wrapped up Lynnie, his shoulder brushed against hers. Diedra stepped aside to let him finish tucking his daughter into her carrier. She followed him downstairs and to the front door. Eli glanced over his shoulder to where she stood silhouetted in the lighted doorway.

"Good night," he called with a wave of his hand.

"Good night." She was still standing there when he turned the corner.

Lynnie slept through the drive. At home he placed her in the crib and turned off the light.

He paused outside the nursery and listened for a moment to see if she stirred. Eli couldn't believe Diedra had offered to come to his house and care for Lynnie. That went far beyond the call of duty.

Her capacity for giving amazed him. Already she lavished it on the kids and senior citizens but still had enough left over to share with him and Lynnie.

If only he could put his grief behind him, she would be the type of woman he could love forever. She would love a man despite his faults. But he wasn't ready. And what would Diedra think if she knew the truth?

six

After he left, Diedra straightened the kitchen and did a few tasks downstairs before locking up and turning out the lights.

Upstairs she ran hot water in the tub and sprinkled in some of her favorite bath salts. She put her favorite Christian music in the player and slid into the fragrant water.

Emotion choked her as the words of one of the songs brought tears. "I'm so sorry, Jesus," she whispered, knowing nothing she had endured could ever be a fraction of what her Lord had suffered on the cross because of His love for her.

After her bath Diedra prepared for bed. She knelt by her bedside and turned to God in prayer, seeking His help for all the burdens on her heart that night. She thought for a moment about Eli's concern for her. What would it have been like to tell him the truth? To share her burden. She might tell herself Eli was only a friend, but she knew things were going beyond that. She was feeling emotions she'd suppressed for so long, but she knew she couldn't lose sight of the way things had to be. She'd spent the past five years trying to forget, trying to trust again.

Eli employed her to provide his daughter with the best of care. And that was all they could ever share. She wouldn't consider love again until she came to grips with the past. Others might think she gave too much, but only she knew how little she could give.

After her "shopping-care" kids left at noon on Saturday, Diedra called Eli.

"How's Lynnie?"

"We spent the early morning hours in the emergency room."

"Oh, Eli. What did the doctor say?"

"She has an ear infection."

"Poor baby. How can I help?"

"There's nothing you can do."

Diedra knew Eli was exhausted but accepted his refusal. "Let me know if I can help."

"Enjoy your night off. You deserve it."

❧

On Sunday Diedra didn't ask if he needed help. She arrived at Eli's after church, using the bottles she'd retrieved and the plate of food from the homecoming meal as excuses to stop by.

Eli met her at the door, cradling the crying baby against his shoulder. He seemed almost desperate when he handed Lynnie over, taking the items she carried and disappearing into the kitchen. Diedra rocked the baby against her shoulder. She cooed soothing words as she reached for her tote bag and pulled out a water bottle.

"What do you plan to do with that?" Eli asked somewhat skeptically as he returned to the room.

"Heat helps. Granny mentioned a warm bag of salt or tea tree oil, but I figured this would be easier. I don't have a clue about the oil."

"I gave her pain medication a few minutes ago."

"Let's try the water bottle. It can't hurt."

Eli heated water and retrieved towels from the linen closet. Diedra wrapped the bottle and maneuvered the baby against the warmth. Lynnie continued to cry. Diedra rubbed her back and whispered words of comfort, praying the medication would take effect soon. She whispered a prayer of thanks when Lynnie calmed down and her eyes drifted closed.

"You think that thing really did the job?" Eli asked.

Diedra shrugged. "Sometimes the old-fashioned remedies work best."

"You mind if I hold on to that until I can buy one?"

"It's yours. I didn't know if you had one, so I picked it up at the drugstore on the way over."

After Lynnie's crisis passed, Diedra felt like a kid in a candy store. The nursery of pink ruffles and lace had everything from a canopied gleaming brass crib to a large wooden carousel horse. "This room is fantastic!" Diedra exclaimed, trying to take in everything at once.

"Lynnie's mom picked out the furnishings. I can't tell you how long we looked for that crib."

"It was worth the effort. This room is so feminine."

Eli reached to turn back the pink-striped comforter. "My baby girl is pretty feminine."

After Diedra laid the baby down, Eli took his time smoothing the covers over her. She stirred when her father kissed her head then settled herself.

He pulled the shades and turned off all the lights except for a tiny night-light; then he pushed a few buttons on a panel by the door. "This activates a monitor wired into the house's sound system. I can hear her wherever I go."

"You've thought of everything," Diedra said. "This room, the monitoring system, even the way you handle her. She's your little princess."

"She sleeps like there's a pea under that mattress," Eli said, his grin turning into a wide yawn.

She laughed. "You need a nap, too. Did you want to eat first?"

He led the way into the kitchen. Diedra caught her breath at the sheer elegance of the room. Lynnie's discomfort had taken priority, so she hadn't paid much attention to her surroundings.

She'd seen rooms like this only in decorator magazines. Her gaze lingered on the stained-glass cabinet doors before moving to the large bay window and the assortment of plants. "You did this?"

He smiled at her. "I own a design and furniture showroom."

"I'm impressed."

Eli retrieved the plate he'd placed in the fridge earlier and removed the foil wrap. "Did you eat?" He put the plate in the microwave.

Diedra nodded. "There was a ton of food at the church."

The microwave timer beeped, and he took the plate to the granite-topped island. Diedra leaned against the counter. "So what can you do with an upstairs apartment in an old Victorian?"

He held up a finger as he chewed and swallowed. "Ah, the potential is boundless. I see a blue-flowered, overstuffed sofa with a matching armchair. Cream walls, hardwood floors."

Diedra laughed as he described her own furnishings. "Exhaustion must have drained your creative genius. Maybe you'll do better after a few hours of sleep."

"Or a few weeks," Eli countered with a grin. He ate a few bites of food and rewrapped the plate. "That's enough for now. Let's go into the sunroom. I'll stretch out in my chair, and we can talk."

Despite his plan to talk, Eli soon dozed off, and as he napped, Diedra struggled to contain her curiosity. She wanted to explore, to learn more about Eli.

Instead, she flipped through a magazine. Being here was important. She knew that. Not even Lynnie's cries woke him. Diedra took care of the baby's needs and comforted her until she drifted off again. The hours stretched into late afternoon, and Diedra would have stayed longer if she hadn't invited

Granny to attend the concert at church with her that night.

Even in his semi-awake state, it took Diedra several minutes to convince Eli to let her and Granny help with Lynnie's care. He relented, but only for one day.

"She's going to be sick for more than a day," Granny argued when Diedra shared the plan with her that evening.

"He knows that, but we have to convince Eli this is not a problem for us. He feels he's taking advantage," Diedra explained at Granny's puzzled expression. "I told him the center is covered, but he only agreed to let you take care of her tomorrow while he sorts out things at work. I wouldn't be surprised if he's home early. He could be feeling guilty about leaving Lynnie when she's sick."

"I'll talk to him and try to make him understand he shouldn't stand in the way of people intent on doing good deeds."

"Do that. And convince him to let me stay with Lynnie on Tuesday," Diedra added.

Granny smiled. "So when are you going to tell me about you and Eli?"

"There's nothing to tell."

"Now you know better than that," Granny told her. "You care a great deal more for Eli McKay than you're letting on."

Diedra shook her head. "I can't. I'll hurt him."

"That's a possibility with any relationship, but if you follow God's leading, I doubt it would happen."

"I'm trying, Granny."

❧

On Monday morning Diedra eyed the pale blue page of the checkbook. Spending money had never seemed less interesting. She needed more coffee before she started on the payroll and bills.

Diedra stood and reached for her mug then sank back into

the chair. At that moment Granny walked into the room carrying a thermal carafe. "Ready for a refill?"

She held out her cup. "You're a lifesaver. Caffeine is the only thing keeping me going."

"Heard from Eli and Lynnie yet?"

"No," Diedra said. "I hate it that she's sick."

"Me, too." Granny closed the cap before setting the carafe on the desktop.

"He should be here any minute. Remember to talk him into letting me stay with Lynnie tomorrow."

"You're needed here. They were telling me just now what Davey's been up to lately. A play for your attention, I suppose."

"How can that be?" Diedra asked, smiling. "Davey spends nearly as much time in my office as I do."

Davey's antics were legendary around the center. Every staff member had a Davey story that topped the one before. Diedra didn't even want to know what he'd done today but knew she'd hear soon enough. "By the way, we have Janice Gore to thank for referring Eli."

"So Eli knows Davey," Granny said.

"They're old pals."

"No doubt Eli figured you could handle anything if you could handle that boy."

She shuffled the papers into a pile then picked up her pen, tapping out a rhythm against the desktop. "Maybe I should ask Janice about Eli."

Granny looked confused. "What exactly are you hoping to find out?"

"I have to know he's trustworthy," Diedra admitted.

"That's something you need to determine for yourself, Dee."

"I don't even know why I feel this way. I'm not sure I believe in love anymore."

"There's too much love in you to allow apathy to rule your feelings toward anyone, including Eli. One day you'll get over what Benjamin did. You'll live and love again."

Diedra wished that could be true. "What man would want me, Granny? I can't give him children. Until I let go of the past, I can't even offer him the love he deserves. It's not fair to ask anyone to wait until I'm ready."

"Fairness rarely has anything to do with falling in love. You know that. You can't fill the loneliness in your heart with the children and old people in this place. A man who loves you would help ease the loneliness. And scars fade in time, just like memories."

"Oh, Granny, I want to believe that."

"You'll see. That's what love's about. Trust God to provide."

How many times would Granny have to remind her to trust God? Diedra believed in God's provisions, but she had so much to work out before she could ever hope to have a normal life. The ringing phone jarred the silence in the room. "Kids Unlimited."

"Dee, it's Eli."

"Hi. How's Lynnie?"

"We're leaving the doctor's office now. He gave us antibiotics and eardrops. Guess that means we won't have to find that oil you told me about."

Diedra laughed. "I could ask Granny if she has any. Did she wake again last night?"

"Around two. Is Mrs. Wright there now?"

Diedra winked at the older woman. "She's right here. What time will you pick her up?"

"Ten minutes," Eli said. "I won't bring Lynnie in."

"I'll have Granny meet you outside."

"Are you sure she'll be okay?"

"Without a doubt. What about you? Don't you need to rest before you go to work?"

Eli's sigh sounded slightly regretful. "I wish. If I weren't up to my neck right now, I'd stay home with Lynnie."

"It'll be okay," Diedra assured him softly. "Ten minutes then."

Diedra watched Granny hurry away to collect her belongings. Her cheerful bustle, much like when she helped around the center, assured Diedra one of them had something to look forward to that day.

It took all of her willpower to stay in her chair and wave good-bye to Granny a few minutes later. She wouldn't even look out the window. No matter how much she wanted to see Eli and Lynnie.

"Got a minute?"

Diedra's heart flip-flopped at the sound of Eli's voice. "Sure. I thought you weren't coming in," she said, happiness warming her from the inside out.

"I just wanted to say thanks for everything."

Diedra's heart thumped wildly. *Fairness rarely has anything to do with falling in love.* The words seemed to rebound through the room. *Don't be silly,* she chided herself. But there was no denying the truth. She cared a great deal for Eli McKay.

"Do you feel better about Lynnie? Did you ask the doctor about the late-night sessions?"

Eli nodded. "He agrees with you. Thinks getting her back on schedule will take care of those episodes." He glanced at his watch. "I have a ten o'clock appointment. I need to drop them off at the house."

"I'll stop by later and check on them if you want."

"You don't have time," he pointed out.

"It's no problem. Honestly."

"We went over this yesterday," Eli said.

"What if I charge you? Would that make it better?"

He chuckled. "I suppose it would seem less like taking advantage."

"My price is ten minutes of your daughter's time." Diedra smiled. "Payable upon arrival, of course."

Eli laughed. "It's a deal. I have to run. Mrs. Wright will think I got lost."

Bemused, Diedra lifted her hand then let it drop. She was teetering on a crazy emotional seesaw, but Sarah pulled her back to earth when she entered the office with one of the children from her classroom.

"What's up?"

"Eddie and Davey are fighting over a quarter."

"It's mine," Eddie said, breaking into tears. "I got it for my tooth. See?" He indicated the gap in the front of his mouth.

"How did Davey get your money?"

"I lost it. Davey says finders keepers, but it's mine."

The tears fell even faster, and Diedra knelt to hug the child. "It's okay, sweetie. We'll find your quarter." She slipped her hand into her pocket and fingered the coins before coming across the right change. "Here—let me look behind your ear. Maybe you lost it there."

Eddie shook his head. "It was in my pocket."

"Well, perhaps it slipped out. Why, look here," she cried as she fingered his hair. "Here's a quarter."

"Where?" Eddie demanded, squirming to see when she pulled the coin from behind his ear. Diedra showed him, and his sad eyes brightened.

He reached for the money. "I'm going to put it in my bank."

"Why don't you let me keep it for now?" Diedra held out

her hand. "We wouldn't want it to get lost behind your ear again." Taking his hand, she led him over to the desk and placed the money in the wooden box that sat there. "See—I'll keep it right here for you."

Eddie nodded and wrapped his arms around her legs.

Diedra hugged him again. She glanced at Sarah. "I'll walk down with you and talk to Davey."

Sarah reached for Eddie's hand.

Davey denied having Eddie's quarter, and Diedra decided to let the matter drop for now and talk to his mother that afternoon.

After leaving the classroom, Diedra made her way to the nursery. "Hi, Gina," she said, plucking Timmy from the crib.

"Busy morning?"

Diedra sat in a rocker and accepted the bottle Gina handed her. She settled Timmy in her arms, enjoying the baby smell of him as she fed him. "You know, it just occurred to me that Davey starts school next fall. What will we do for excitement around here?"

"He's probably been training Kaylie."

Diedra laughed and nodded, her gaze touching on the baby who moved around on the play mats. "Please tell me he started crawling at home."

Gina settled in the rocker next to hers with a baby and bottle. "His mom's delighted. She thinks the other babies inspired him."

Diedra felt relieved. Too many times parents experienced guilt when they missed a milestone in their children's lives.

"How's Lynnie?" Gina asked.

"Ear infection."

"So we won't be seeing the gorgeous Mr. McKay this week?"

"Lynnie may be back later in the week."

"So Mr. McKay did make his daily stop by the director's office this morning?"

Diedra looked at Gina. "He's checking on his daughter."

"Funny. He always asks me how she's doing," Gina pointed out, her eyes twinkling.

"That's because I pay you to tell him," Diedra said. She lifted Timmy to her shoulder, and he rewarded her with a resounding burp. "You need something to occupy your time with this cushy job."

Both women laughed at the absurdity of Diedra's statement and settled the babies in their cribs.

"I'll be back later," Diedra said.

She took advantage of a lull in activity to run by Eli's house. She rang the doorbell and studied the outside of his home. Not a mansion but definitely not a cottage either. The painted woodwork gleamed in the sunlight. The lawns and shrubbery were meticulous, not a fallen leaf in sight.

"Hello, Granny," Diedra said, kissing the woman's cheek in greeting before she lifted Lynnie from her arms. "How's she doing?"

"She seems comfortable for now."

Granny poured two glasses of soda, and they sat and talked while Diedra played with Lynnie. The time passed quickly. "I'd better get back to work," she announced reluctantly as she transferred Lynnie into Granny's arms. Diedra smoothed a hand over the baby's head and squeezed Granny's arm gently. "Call if you need me."

"I will. Thanks for checking on us."

"You're too smart for your own good," Diedra told her.

Granny laughed. "Have a good afternoon."

Back at the center Diedra recalled Gina's teasing about Eli's daily visits. The woman had been right. Eli did make an effort to see her every day. She would miss not seeing him while Lynnie was out sick.

Don't do this to yourself, Diedra cautioned. She knew exactly where self-examination would lead. She picked up the day's mail and found that the licensing packet had arrived. She needed to help Gina with the babies again, and then she would find time to read the information. She still had to check next week's menus, order supplies, and contact a couple of parents.

As Diedra worked, her thoughts drifted back to what she'd asked Granny that morning. What harm would it do to ask Janice about Eli? Just a conversation between two friends. Eli would never know. Janice had to collect Davey's quarter anyway.

The phone rang, and Diedra felt guilty when Eli's voice filled her ear.

"Glad I caught you. It looks as if I'm going to be an hour late getting home. You aren't going to charge me sixty dollars, are you?" Eli asked, speaking of the dollar-a-minute late charge.

"I can't charge you, but you need to see if Granny can stay."

"I'd better call and ask."

"Talk to you later," Diedra said, glancing up at the tap on the door. She waved Janice in.

"Diedra!" Eli called just as she started to hang up. She pulled the receiver back to her ear. "Come over for dinner tonight. I can fix something, or we can order in."

"Okay. See you around seven."

Diedra focused on replacing the receiver before meeting Janice's smile. "Eli."

"So I gathered. Sarah said you wanted to see me. You aren't giving Davey his walking papers, I hope?"

"No, nothing like that," Diedra said. "There is something about Davey, but I had another matter I wanted to discuss with you."

Janice let out a sigh as she sank into a chair, resting her hand against her heart. "You take five years off my life every time you summon me to your office. I feel as if I'm going to the principal's office. As long as Davey's secure, go ahead."

"What can you tell me about Eli?"

"Probably no more than you already know," Janice said, shaking her head. "He's handsome, charming, well respected in his business, and adores his child. I wish I could tell you more."

The feelings of guilt returned. What on earth had made her think Janice could enlighten her? "I'm sorry, Janice. I shouldn't have put you on the spot like that."

"Never be sorry for caring for someone, particularly Eli. I think you're good for him. I know you care about him."

"Janice. . ."

"Don't deny your feelings, Diedra. Caring is one of your best traits, but you have to allow people to care for you in return."

If only she could share how difficult it was for her to let people get close. Children were different. Every one of them stole away a little of her heart, but they gave so much more in return.

The thought of giving her heart to another person incapable of returning her love scared Diedra. "What I really need to discuss with you is Davey's quarter."

Janice frowned. "Davey doesn't have a quarter. We never allow him to bring money to day care."

Diedra explained the situation then summoned Davey to the office.

"Do you have Eddie's quarter?" Janice asked her son.

Davey produced the coin from the tiny watch pocket of his jeans. "I found it."

Janice took the money from his hand and gave it to Diedra. "You knew it belonged to Eddie. What you did was wrong, Davey. We don't ever make other people cry." Janice stood and captured his hand. "We'll see what your dad has to say about the matter."

After they left, Diedra found herself thinking about the life lesson that had transpired in her office. She wished Janice's claim to her son that "we don't ever make other people cry" could be true. The world would certainly be a better place.

Janice had forced her to face another truth—one she fought to deny. She cared a great deal for Eli. A myriad of emotions filled Diedra with the truth—fear, excitement, and a tremendous anxiety. What would happen if she allowed herself to love Eli? Would doing so bring pain or untold joy? Was she willing to take the chance?

seven

Eli paced the living room, looking out the full-length glass windows every time a car drove down the street. He waited for Diedra, and despite his apprehension, Eli knew he wanted her there with him.

He'd gone inside the center that morning for one reason. He didn't want to go through a day without seeing her. And he'd invited her to dinner for the same reason. He wanted—no, he needed—to spend time with her.

Headlights flooded the room as a car pulled into the driveway. "Act your age, man. You're not some sixteen-year-old who's never dated," he muttered, rubbing his sweaty palms on his jeans.

Eli jerked the door open and watched Diedra approach. She'd changed into jeans and a furry pastel pink sweater. She smiled, and the doubts evaporated.

"Get all your charges home safely?" he asked, returning her smile. She nodded, and he invited her inside. "I'm glad you came. I wish we could have gone out to dinner."

Diedra set her bag on the small bench in the foyer, her keys jangling as she dropped them inside. "This is better. You don't have to worry with a sitter. Did I tell you I love your home?"

Eli enjoyed the way she assessed the room. He'd seen the look often when his customers fell in love with a piece of furniture or room arrangement. "After the initial shock, you mean?"

She laughed. "I had no idea you were so talented. Are these original pieces?"

"They're one-of-a-kind pieces. I designed everything here exclusively for myself."

"It's a great showroom." Diedra glanced at him. "Don't your buyers want similar designs?"

"They don't see these," Eli explained. "I'm fortunate my business associates understand it's easier for me to have dinner parties at restaurants."

Diedra pointed to the oval stained-glass window. "Where did you find that?"

"I made it."

Her mouth dropped open. "It's fabulous."

"Thanks." He lifted his shoulders and stared moodily at the piece. The window had been the largest item he'd ever done. A flower garden in glass, his instructor had called it.

He'd been so depressed after Kelly's death that his doctor suggested Eli take up a hobby to help work through his emotions. And it had helped. The creative pieces had passed the time, vented his frustrations, and left him this memento to show that sometimes beauty comes from pain. "I need to take Mrs. Wright home, and I—"

"Granny's still here?" Diedra asked.

He nodded. "In the nursery."

"I'll go say hello."

Not ready to share her yet, Eli wrapped his fingers lightly about Diedra's wrist. He noted the way she stiffened then relaxed in his hold. "I thought if you stayed with Lynnie, I could pick up dinner on my way back."

Diedra looped her arm through his and urged him toward the nursery. "Sounds good."

Eli watched as she kissed Granny Marie's cheek and fingered Lynnie's curls. The older woman said something, and Diedra's soft laughter filled the room.

You've got it bad, old man, Eli thought. Diedra touched his life in ways he hadn't thought he'd experience again—her concern for Lynnie, Granny, the children in the center, even him.

"Eli's picking up supper. Want to stay?" Diedra issued the invitation then glanced at Eli and smiled.

He returned her smile. Inviting Granny wasn't his choice, but if Diedra wanted the woman to stay, he wouldn't refuse her.

"No, thank you," Granny said, careful not to disturb the sleeping baby as she put her in the crib. "Francie's already upset because I didn't rush home tonight."

Eli noted Diedra's dismayed expression. "Who is Francie?" he asked.

Diedra turned to him. "Her daughter-in-law." Then she looked at Granny Marie. "Why didn't you say something earlier?"

"Jimmy knows where I am, and Francie needs to learn things don't always go as planned."

No, they don't, Eli agreed, thinking her words sounded almost prophetic. He and Diedra had been trying to arrange their relationship on their own terms, but he had the feeling God planned to move it along a completely different path.

"You'd better get me home, Eli." Granny tucked the covers about Lynnie then folded a blanket, placing it over the back of the rocker.

"Wait," Diedra said. "Let me tell you what Davey did today. But let's go downstairs so we don't disturb Lynnie."

❧

Both Granny and Eli chuckled over Davey's latest stunt as they left the house. Diedra waved and closed the door.

She paused in the living room, the stained glass catching her attention, then walked over to examine it more closely. A work of art, filled with talent and emotion. Yet somehow

Eli seemed unimpressed by his accomplishment.

Diedra checked on Lynnie again and decided to wait in the sunroom. The darkening shadows of the late fall evening showed through the glass walls. She flipped a wall switch and flooded the backyard with light. A large expanse of deck stretched across the back of the house next to a covered pool.

Another switch lit the lamps. This room fascinated her the most. Unlike the rest of the house, the eclectic mixture of modern furniture and antiques made the room a place where people lived. Again an abundance of healthy plants dotted the room along with exquisite pewter figurines and china plates. Walls of bookcases overflowed with a mixture of leather-bound collector's editions, popular hardcover fiction, action-adventure paperbacks, and volumes on furniture and antique history. Diedra trailed her finger along the spines, stopping on the ones of formula car racing.

A photo of a man in some sort of zippered suit sat on the bookcase. She lifted the carved wood frame to examine the photo in detail. A helmet made it impossible to tell who leaned against the formula car, his fingers forming a victory sign. Maybe someone Eli knew. Perhaps this explained his interest in racing.

Puzzled, Diedra replaced the photo and moved to the collection on the sofa table. There were several with Eli as a member of a group. Probably his parents, she decided upon seeing a resemblance between him and the older man in the photo. One of him in a porch swing with a beautiful woman caught her eye. Diedra reached for the silver frame.

Could this be Kelly? They looked so in love. Her fingers trembled as she replaced the picture and managed to knock over another. As she set it upright, she found the photo that told her all she needed to know about Eli McKay.

Apparently it was a recent shot, for the photographer had captured Eli's contentment as he presented Lynnie to the camera with happiness so real it stole Diedra's breath. She knew he loved his child, but she hadn't realized to what degree.

"There you are."

She screamed, stifling the sound with a hand over her mouth when she whirled to find Eli standing behind her. "That was quick."

"I know the shortcuts."

"I remembered this room from Sunday night. I thought it might be where you spend your evenings."

"This mishmash of design is my favorite room in the house. Both Kelly and I loved to read. The pewter pieces belonged to my dad, and the china plates belonged to Kelly's family."

"And someone definitely has a green thumb."

"I love plants. I never feel a room is complete without them. Are you ready to eat?"

"Let me wash up, and I'll meet you in the kitchen."

She stopped by the nursery to check on Lynnie. Diedra smoothed the blanket over her tiny form and watched for a second longer before going downstairs.

Eli had spread the meal over the kitchen island and settled on a stool. Diedra sat across from him. "Lynnie's resting comfortably. I'm so glad she's doing better."

"Probably resting up to give her daddy one tough time tonight," Eli said. "I hope you like Chinese."

"Love it. I never know exactly what I'm eating, though."

"I'm a Chinese takeout expert. I ordered wontons, chicken and broccoli, beef with green peppers, sweet and sour pork, egg rolls, and fried rice," he said, indicating cartons as he ticked through the list. "I wasn't sure what you liked."

"I know I've ordered one or two of those items. But how many people did you plan to feed?"

"One very hungry man and one little lady who looks as if she can't eat very much."

"You'd be surprised," Diedra said.

Eli asked a blessing on the food, thanking the Lord for His continued care for him, Lynnie, and Diedra.

"Thank you," she told him, accepting the carton Eli passed her way. "I appreciate your adding me to your prayer list."

"I hope I'm on yours, too," Eli said.

Diedra nodded. "Oh, look—it's a full moon," she whispered as the brightness filtered into the room.

"I ordered that today," Eli teased, bringing a ready smile to her face. "Right after you agreed to have dinner with me."

"I'm glad you did."

"Order the full moon?" Eli asked, his gaze lingering on her until Diedra dropped her head, feeling about as shy as Lynnie.

"No—invite me to dinner."

"I'm glad, too. Now try these wontons. They're the best I've ever eaten."

Eli kept the conversation flowing as they ate. His comment of how much he appreciated Granny Marie's help reminded Diedra of the older woman's home situation. "I hope Granny and Francie got everything sorted out."

Eli nodded. "I didn't want to say anything in front of Granny Marie, but I thought you said it wouldn't be a problem."

Diedra didn't know what to say. "It wasn't supposed to be. I think Granny and her daughter-in-law experience conflicts when Francie tries to control Granny's life."

"She offered to come back tomorrow, but I don't want to get in the middle of a family conflict."

"I'm sorry, Eli. I'm sure they've worked things out. So tell me—who's the race fan? I noticed the books."

His jaw tensed. "I raced formula cars until last year. I started right after I finished college."

The driver in the photo is Eli. An ever-changing mystery, he'd just revealed something she'd never have guessed. Diedra tried to cover her shock. "You miss it, don't you?"

"At times."

"Why did you quit?"

"Driving was all I ever wanted to do. After Kelly died and Lynnie was born, I knew I had to give it up. I'd rather not talk about this."

"You should," she insisted.

"Quitting was my choice. There's too much risk. My daughter needs her father."

His stance tugged at Diedra's heartstrings. All her life she had wished for a man who put his family before everything else. Now she'd found one and knew she should run the other way, but she couldn't.

"I have to establish security for my child. I want to be around to see her grow up. I refuse to make Lynnie worry the way Kelly and my parents did."

Diedra laid her fork on the plate and looked at him. "I think you're a very special man, Eli McKay."

"Do you mean that, Dee?"

She found his intense regard unsettling.

"Dee?"

She nodded, managing a shaky smile. "Yes. Telling myself to keep this strictly business is not working. I'm not sure I can deal with this right now."

"You're going to have to, aren't you?"

Diedra tried to tell him the truth but found she couldn't.

Lynnie's cries echoed over the speaker system. His daughter had a knack of crying right on cue.

"I'll take care of her," Eli said. "Eat. We'll discuss this when I get back."

Anxiety replaced hunger. She couldn't allow this situation to go any further. Diedra hurried to the living room, her movements almost furtive as she picked up her purse and started toward the door.

"Where are you going?" Eli asked as she laid her hand on the doorknob.

"I thought I'd go home. . . ." Her voice faded to a hushed stillness.

"You're not going anywhere until we talk," he said.

"Lynnie needs you."

"She's fussing in her sleep. We need to talk."

"I can't." Diedra fidgeted with her purse strap.

"Why did you accept my dinner invitation?" Eli asked.

"Because. . ." She should never have come here tonight, particularly after realizing how she felt about him. He deserved more than she could give.

"The first time we met, I looked you in the eye and knew right then that you would play an important role in my life." He paused as if considering his next words carefully. "I've grieved for Kelly and known I couldn't afford to get too close. But I couldn't deny I wanted to be near you. I used Lynnie as an excuse to see you, and you didn't discourage me."

Diedra started to protest but accepted that he told the truth. She didn't confer with other parents on a daily basis. Only Eli. They shared a spark that had flamed despite their combined efforts to extinguish it. She nodded.

"What are we going to do?" he asked softly.

"I don't know," she said. "I've never become involved with

an enrollee's father before. I'm not even sure it's good business sense."

"This isn't business, Dee. This is you and me and this new experience we're sharing." He moved around the sofa. "We have time to get to know each other better, see where it leads. That is, if you're interested."

Her eyes closed. She wanted to believe love was a possibility for them.

"What do you want, Dee?"

What did she want? *Please, God, help me,* she prayed silently.

"Diedra?"

A battle raged within Diedra. She longed to say yes, but she knew that wouldn't be fair to Eli. She wrung her hands in frustration.

"I never should have let things go this far. You should go, Diedra. It's late, and tomorrow's another early day."

She gasped, her eyes widening. Eli had made the decision for her. He'd taken her silence to mean no.

eight

The enormity of Eli's words hit Diedra hard when he stormed from the room. He'd suggested they see what the future held for them, and she'd upset him with her silence.

Dazed, Diedra felt the sudden need to do something. Back in the kitchen she closed the cartons and placed the leftovers in the refrigerator.

A wry smile touched her lips. Maybe she should just disappear into the dark without a word. In the end that would be best for them both.

Several minutes passed before Eli returned. "I thought you'd be gone."

She scraped her plate into the garbage disposal.

"Look, Diedra. It would be better if you left. You're right to avoid further involvement with me. I'm not over Kelly's death. I might never stop grieving for what I've lost."

His face, tight with suffering, mobilized her into action. "You have a right to grieve for the woman you loved. She was a part of you. She's a part of your child. No woman who loves you will ever expect you to forget Kelly."

"Then why did you hesitate?"

"It's a trust issue for me, Eli," she said. "I'm afraid to let go. Afraid of what will happen if I do."

"You can trust me, Dee. I wouldn't hurt you."

"I hope not. That's why I stayed. I want you to know—"

Lynnie's cries interrupted her, filling the room.

"What's that old adage about children being seen and not

heard?" Eli seemed disgruntled by his daughter's poor timing.

"I'll get her," Diedra volunteered.

"I'll warm a bottle."

The night-light provided sufficient illumination for Diedra to see that Lynnie was awake. "Hey, sweetie," she whispered.

Lynnie rewarded her by kicking her legs in recognition and reaching out to her. She lifted the baby and carried her to the changing table. Afterward Diedra smoothed the long gown over her legs. "You're a blessed little girl," she cooed, cuddling the infant against her chest. "Your daddy sure does love you. And I think I love him, too."

The truth stunned Diedra. She did love Eli. She loved everything about him—his kindness, his loving nature, his dedication to his child and business, all the things that made up the man he was.

"Diedra?"

"Coming," she called.

Eli met her in the hallway, and they walked into the sunroom. She placed Lynnie in his arms. "I checked her temperature. It's normal."

As he became more focused on his daughter, Diedra felt in the way. "I should go," she said.

"Stay." He tugged her down on the sofa beside them. Time slipped away as they spent the remainder of the evening on the sofa talking. Eli told her about his wife and parents. Content to listen, Diedra didn't share her personal story. As the hour grew late, she noted Eli's exhaustion and Lynnie's wide-eyed alertness. She glanced at her watch. "It's almost one o'clock."

"I feel guilty for keeping you here so long. You have a day with the kids ahead of you. I was selfish."

"I could have left," she said. "I enjoyed this evening."

He squeezed her hand. "Me, too."

Eli followed Diedra to the foyer. She picked up her purse and turned the deadbolt on the front door, swinging it open.

"Good night," Eli said, kissing her gently. "I'll call you."

He stood in the doorway with Lynnie as Diedra walked along the lighted path to her car. Feeling the late night chill, she hurried. Diedra turned the ignition and waited for the engine to warm up.

Eli had said he'd call her. Those three words could be the kiss of death to a relationship. How would she feel if Eli didn't call? Was she strong enough to face the disappointment?

Diedra had loved only one man, her husband. She'd accepted that Benjamin hadn't known how to love. She'd tried to show him how, and he'd beat the desire out of her. Now she felt nothing but shame for being so weak-willed, for not standing up to him before he killed their child.

Her baby. What would Eli think when she told him she couldn't have babies? Would he understand? Diedra battled the emotions that tore at her. Fear of his reaction when he learned the truths she hid overshadowed the happiness of knowing he cared for her.

It didn't matter anyway. She loved Eli. She always would. But she could never marry him. She'd never deny him the family he wanted. The family he deserved.

Putting the car in reverse, Diedra glanced at the house once more before backing down the driveway. "Lord, help them both get some rest," she prayed as she drove down the empty street.

❧

"It's going to be a long day," Diedra muttered at nine thirty, rubbing her gritty eyes. "Very long." If only she could slip upstairs for a nap. Or just lay her head on the desk. Maybe they wouldn't need her for thirty seconds or so. Her eyes drifted shut then jerked open when the telephone rang. Diedra groped for the receiver. "Yes? Kids Unlimited."

"Diedra?" Granny asked. "Are you okay?"

"Fine, Granny. How's Lynnie?"

"Better," the older woman said. "She must have slept badly last night, though. Eli seemed a little bleary-eyed." She paused. "So how was your date?"

Diedra felt guilty. Why had she done this to herself? To Eli? He didn't know of her self-doubts, of the hatred she felt for one man and at times for herself.

"Diedra?" Granny said when she didn't respond. "I didn't mean to pry."

"You weren't, Granny. How's Lynnie?"

"I told you she's better. Are you sure you're okay?"

"I'm fine. Eli and I talked last night. There are some things to be sorted through."

"What does that mean?" Granny asked.

"We care for each other," Diedra admitted. "Eli wants to see where it leads. But how can I do that to him?"

"Give it to God, then take it one day at a time, Dee. Get to know Eli. When the time is right, share your confidences and let Eli make the decision about what's right for him."

"I don't know, Granny. It doesn't seem fair to go any further without telling him the truth."

"Are you ready to tell him about Benjamin?"

"I can't. Not yet."

She heard Granny sigh. "I'm praying for you, Dee."

The unspoken disappointment in the older woman's tone weighed on Diedra almost as much as her own disappointment at not being able to tell Eli the truth. "What about you and Francie? Did you work things out?" Diedra asked.

There was silence on the other end of the phone. Finally,

Granny asked, "Does your offer for a roommate still stand?"

"You know it does," she said without hesitation.

"I want you to take some time to think about this first, Dee." Granny paused. "I don't want to burden you. I want your life to go on as if I weren't there."

"You could never be a burden. Now tell me what happened."

"Francie became very upset when I got home last night. She'd planned on my bathing the kids and putting them to bed while she prepared dinner for her guests. I didn't say anything until she started accusing me of caring more for others than for my son and grandchildren. I don't need that in my life. I'm a grown woman. I was married for forty-nine years, ran my own home, did volunteer work at my church, and managed to raise a son. I love them all, but I don't want to live with that kind of treatment or be in their way."

Diedra hurt for Granny. She knew things had to be bad for Granny to take action. "How did Jimmy take the news?"

Silence stretched over the distance. "He didn't have a lot to say last night. We had a private discussion this morning. I explained what I plan to do."

"Did he understand?"

"I think so," Granny said. "I told him that's why I went into the rehab center in the first place. I can take care of myself, Diedra. I know I can."

"We'll take care of each other, Granny."

"That we will. I need to go now. The oven timer just went off."

"What are you doing?" Diedra asked.

"Baking Eli an apple pie."

Diedra laughed. "How do you know he likes apple pie?"

"Everybody likes apple pie. Take care, sweetheart."

Granny probably had Eli's dinner planned, house cleaned,

and clothes washed and ironed. Without thinking she picked up the phone and dialed his direct office number, surprised to hear Janice's voice.

"Hi, Diedra. Eli's out front with a customer. Is it an emergency?"

"I can wait," Diedra said, leaning forward in her chair and tapping her fingers against the desktop. "You'll be happy to know Davey's been on his best behavior this morning."

Janice laughed. "Look out, afternoon. Then again I think his father made an impression on him Friday night, and he'll behave for a day or two. Here's Eli now. See you later."

Eli's voice came over the phone. "Hi. What's up?"

"Granny just called—"

"Is Lynnie okay?"

"Lynnie's fine," Diedra assured him. "Granny called to tell me she's moving in with me."

"Are you sure that's a smart move? I don't think it's wise to get involved in family situations. What will you accomplish by offering her an opportunity to separate from her family? This could even cause a bigger rift in their relationship."

How could he question her when he had no idea of the true situation? "Granny's unhappy. Not being a burden to her family and managing her time will make her happy again."

"Are you sure? She's regaining that happiness at what cost? Alienating her son? Her daughter-in-law?"

"No. She's explained her decision to her son. She won't go back to her own home out of respect for him. He doesn't want her living alone."

"With reason, I'm sure."

"She's doing much better," Diedra insisted. Eli's disapproval disappointed her. "There's no basis for him to monitor her every breath."

"And what about her son's need to care for his aging mother? How can he do that if he's eliminated from the picture?"

"Granny and I have given the matter lots of thought and prayer, Eli. She needs her independence."

"I'm not sure why you feel you have to do this, but I get the impression there's more to the situation than meets the eye."

"Don't analyze me," Diedra snapped.

"I'm just suggesting you don't take a step you'll regret later," he said.

"I won't have regrets. Granny is my friend. I look forward to sharing my home with her."

"I'm not trying to pick a fight, Dee."

"You're criticizing me."

"And you're being defensive," he countered. "Friends give each other advice. I'm advising you to rethink your plans before you get hurt."

"I have to go," she said abruptly.

"I'll see you this afternoon."

She didn't respond.

"We are going to see each other again, aren't we, Diedra?"

The old fears and uncertainties loomed in her mind.

"Dee?"

"I don't know." The confusion-filled words came out in a rush. Last night had been a different place and time. She needed time to reorient herself, time he wouldn't give her.

"You're not upset because I don't agree with what you're doing, are you? Your life is going to change in a big way because of this decision. I just want you to understand how big."

"I expected support, not criticism. I shared good news with you, and you've turned it into the biggest mistake I've ever made in my life."

"I'm not going to tell you it's a great idea. If you thought I'd made a bad decision, you'd tell me, wouldn't you?"

"You already made that mistake getting involved with me."

"Why would you say something like that?" he asked, his voice agitated.

Granny's position hadn't changed. She needed help, and Diedra had to help her. "I have to go. Good-bye, Eli."

❧

"Diedra?" he said into the receiver, only to find she'd hung up.

No matter how much he tried to understand her, he always ended up more confused. What did she mean that he'd made a mistake by getting involved with her? What was she hiding from him? Why was she pushing him away?

The worn leather chair tilted backward, the squeaking springs unnoticed as he lapsed into thought. He needed time to get to know Diedra, to learn all about her—her past, her dreams for the future. He needed to know what made her smile, what excited her, what caused her to be happy or sad. He wanted to eliminate the sadness from her life. He didn't want her to cry because of him.

Love made a person vulnerable, opened them to hurt. In one way he could understand she was upset because he hadn't shared her excitement. But he saw the other side of the situation. He understood the potential for pain for Granny Marie and her family.

Eli reached for the phone. He'd call her back. See if they could work things out. Before he could dial, he heard a sharp rap on his office door. "Come in!"

His secretary opened the door and stepped inside. "Janice needs you right away."

Eli paused by the desk. He wanted to call Diedra first.

"Eli." Janice entered the room. "We have 'enraged' times two out here."

Frustrated, he followed Janice into the hallway. Diedra would understand. Business came first for her, too.

❧

Diedra stared at the phone as if willing it to ring would make things different. It wouldn't, and if anyone should know it, she should.

Benjamin Pierce had been self-centered to the core. Charismatic, handsome, everything she'd ever dreamed of in a man. Or so she thought. She married him, unaware of the problems he'd buried beneath the polish. He thought only of himself. Especially the times when he used her as a punching bag.

Desperate, she'd gone to her father, only to have him insist she stop her foolishness and return home. When Benjamin nearly killed her, her parents didn't want their precious name connected with scandal.

Diedra could think only of herself. She could accept his love and keep her secret. But she knew they both would lose in the end.

She could never do that to Eli. The first loving, giving man she'd ever known had been hurt too much for her to add to his pain. Let him remain angry with her. It would be best for them both in the long run.

Diedra wiped away the tear that trickled down her cheek. Before, she'd gone to counseling and managed to pick up the pieces and put herself back together. Then she'd had her grandparents. This time she had God. She would do it again. She still had her children, her center, and her best friend.

nine

Eli's gaze went immediately to the wall clock when he returned to his office. He couldn't believe it had taken two hours to placate the Albrittons. From experience, though, he knew they would probably decide they wanted a completely different design.

He needed to see Diedra. He refused to allow her to push him out of her life without his understanding why. Eli reached for the phone, propping it against the desk as he punched the numbers. He put the receiver back in the cradle. He couldn't make her understand on the phone. This required a face-to-face, look-her-in-the-eye discussion.

During the drive, Eli went back over Diedra's words, looking for something at odds with the woman he thought he knew. Last night she had been receptive to furthering their relationship. Today she wanted to put it on hold until she tied everything up in tidy little bundles. He had to know what had changed.

Eli opened the door to Diedra's office and stepped inside. He should have called first, but an advance warning would have given her time to raise her guard. Diedra sat at her desk, her eyes closed and her shoulders slumped as though the weight of the world rested there. "Dee?" he said anxiously.

"Eli?" She sat up straighter. "Shouldn't you be home?"

"I called Granny."

"What did you say?" she asked sharply.

Eli hesitated. "That I had work to handle. I wouldn't tell her

I don't agree with what you're doing. It's not my business."

"Oh," she muttered uneasily.

Eli eyed the top of her head. "We need to talk."

She refused to look at him and flicked imaginary specks of dust from her desk. "You really think it's that simple?"

Just apologize, Eli told himself as her words rang in his ears. "You're pushing me away, Diedra. Don't run away from us."

"We're moving too fast, Eli."

He ached to lift her head and look into her eyes. "Then we'll slow down. Just give us a chance. I won't lie to you. Nothing about our relationship will be simple, but we've come a long way since we met. We can handle this."

He watched her, both in anticipation and dread. The sudden tenderness and fierce love he felt startled him.

"I don't know. You're the father of one of my kids," she argued weakly. "And Granny Marie is important to me. I can't risk making her feel unwanted."

"She's not your responsibility."

Diedra frowned. "I invited her to move in with me months ago. Can you imagine how she'd feel if I refused her now? Particularly since she's had a blowup with her daughter-in-law that involves me."

Asking her not to care was like asking a leopard to change his spots. Eli reached out to her in an instinctive gesture of comfort. "It's not my choice to make. I'm sorry I hurt you. Will you forgive me?"

❧

Eli waited for her answer. *Tell him why you can't,* her heart urged. She wasn't ready. Not yet.

Diedra knew her attempts at breaking away would never work as long as they saw each other daily, as long as Eli intended that they wouldn't.

He moved around the desk and pulled her to her feet, encircling her with his arms and pressing a kiss on her forehead. "I had to see you. Will you come to the house after you finish here?"

Diedra knew she should say no. Everything in her said this wasn't right. But she couldn't. "All right."

She followed him onto the porch, watching long after he'd pulled away from the curb. She wrapped her jacket tighter as a sudden chill struck her; she stared into the darkness.

Could love sustain them through her doubts and fears? Without intending to, she'd made a commitment to their future. Her vow not to become involved shattered the moment she saw him. She turned to go back inside.

She loved Eli. But that didn't make her any less afraid. She couldn't postpone her day of reckoning forever. Each passing moment drew her closer to the time she would have to tell him the truth.

Diedra pushed the idea aside and went upstairs to change. She wanted to look beautiful for him and pulled out one of her favorite dresses. She showered, dried her hair, and slipped into the garment. After one last look in the mirror, she dabbed on her best perfume. Downstairs she picked up her coat and purse and headed for Eli's.

The heavy traffic demanded her attention. She was relieved to see the sign for Eli's subdivision.

Lights blazed throughout his house. Ringing the doorbell, Diedra listened for the sound of footsteps on the marble entry hall. The door swung open, and Granny greeted her with a smile. "You're looking extra pretty tonight."

Diedra shrugged. "Oh, I just felt like it."

Granny frowned. "Don't try to fool an old woman, Dee." Then she smiled. "I've never seen you so radiant."

She felt as transparent as glass. "Oh, Granny, I care for him so much it scares me."

"Will you tell him about Benjamin?"

Diedra drew in a deep breath. "I can't. I'll lose him."

"Don't keep secrets. They destroy a relationship faster than anything else."

"I'll tell him soon," Diedra promised.

"I suppose you know best." She turned toward the hallway. "Eli had better get me home. I don't want a repeat of last night's scene."

"You could move in with me tonight," Diedra offered.

"Francie may whine a bit, but I can always start packing."

"I'm sorry it's come to this, Granny."

"Me, too, Diedra. I don't want to come between Jimmy and Francie. I'm depending on you to see that I don't come between you and Eli either."

"Let's cross that bridge when we get to it," Diedra said. "What do I smell? Fried chicken?"

"I cooked supper. Lynnie's doing much better. I think she'll be ready to come back to the center next week."

"I'm sure Eli appreciates everything."

Eli walked up, smiling. "He's forever in her debt." He kissed Diedra. "I'll be back in fifteen minutes."

With her back to Eli, Granny raised her eyebrows and winked then hugged Diedra before stepping through the door. Eli reached over and squeezed her hand as he walked out the door.

Diedra went to check on Lynnie. The baby slept on her stomach, her bottom pushed up in the air. She envied Eli his daughter. He could watch her grow and benefit from her love. He'd rejoice with her in her successes and provide his shoulder to cry on in crises.

Tears welled in Diedra's eyes. She had no idea if her baby had been a Lynnie or a Davey. Grief as strong as that which she had felt years ago overwhelmed her.

Some minutes later Eli joined her in the nursery. "What is it, Diedra? Why are you crying?"

Diedra wiped her hands over her cheeks. "She's so beautiful."

"That's no reason to cry," he said, guiding her from the room. His gentleness spoke of his caring.

"You look beautiful. I wish I could take you somewhere special."

"Another time," Diedra said.

"It's a date. I'm starving. I skipped lunch today."

Eli fixed his plate, and Diedra couldn't help but smile at his combination. "Chicken and apple pie?" she asked. "I know Granny has vegetables in those pans."

He waited for her to serve her own plate and pour iced tea. She pulled out a stool at the counter and sat down. He asked a blessing on the food, and she lifted her fork, only to find her hunger had faded.

Eli studied her. "Are you still upset about this afternoon?"

"No."

"I don't have a right to question your decisions. The way I feel about your involvement in Granny's situation isn't going to stop you from doing what you have to do. You've made no secret of that."

Secret. The word left Diedra breathless. She had too many of them. Her gaze dropped to the plate as she idly rearranged the food. *Don't do this to him. . .to yourself,* her mind warned.

Eli reached for her hand. "I sort of understand about Granny, but I can't help thinking you're setting yourself up for hurt."

"You wouldn't do the same?" Diedra asked, looking him in the eye.

He shrugged. "I can't say that I would. What about when you're not there for her anymore? Will you have helped Granny by not encouraging her to work it out with her family?"

"Where am I going?" Diedra asked. "Kids Unlimited is my life, and for as long as I have a home, Granny has one."

"And if we become involved?"

Tell him about Benjamin.

An overwhelming desire to push the truth even deeper seized her. "I'll make that decision when the time is right. I'm not sure about us. There were issues with my marriage." *Don't stop there,* the voice prompted. *Tell him the truth.* She couldn't. Not now.

He looked at her expectantly.

"Trust issues. I know you won't intentionally hurt me, but I'm afraid."

"You were hurt this afternoon when I didn't agree with you," he said in an effort to prove his point. "But you're here now. You trusted me enough to come over tonight. Doesn't that say something to you about us?"

"I'm so confused," she whispered.

He wrapped her in his arms then hugged her tight. "We'll work through this, Diedra. Just trust God. He'll make it right."

After cleaning the kitchen, Eli asked, "Would you like to look at photo albums? I think one of them has my baby pictures." He chuckled.

"I'd love to," Diedra said, glad for an opportunity to change the subject.

"I want to see your albums, too," Eli said.

A momentary look of discomfort crossed her face. How would Eli react to the fact that her memories only focused on the last five years?

ten

They sat on the sofa, half watching a television program as they talked about their plans for the weekend. Eli studied the face he'd come to love. They'd seen each other every night this week. Though at times Diedra seemed content, he knew she struggled with something of gigantic proportions. Was he the issue? Instinct warned him not to push too hard.

"I'm glad tomorrow's Saturday," Eli said. "You have morning and afternoon sessions of shopping care, don't you?"

"Sounds as if you've memorized my brochure," Diedra teased.

"I have to if I want to see you."

She liked it that he'd taken the time to examine her business. Her shopping-care program did well. The center parents and a few others often arranged to bring their children by for a few hours while they ran errands. Diedra yawned widely. She moved from her comfortable position. "Guess that's my cue to hit the road."

"May I take you to dinner tomorrow night?" Eli asked, taking her hand in his.

Guilt was a strange thing. At times it nagged like a persistent child—always in the background no matter how hard she tried to push it away. Every day she loved Eli a little more, but she had no right. She didn't deserve his trust because she hadn't been truthful with him. And someday the old hurts could destroy everything they'd managed to build.

Diedra fought to swallow the bitterness that rose in her

throat. Though she knew she had to tell Eli about her past, she found it easy to forget while in his presence. The moment became very important, and only when they were apart did she promise to do the right thing the next time she saw him.

Diedra let go of his hand then knelt on the floor and peered under the sofa, searching for her missing shoe. "Gina's picking up tomorrow's sessions so I can help Granny move. I don't know how long it will take. I hoped it wouldn't take more than two or three trips with the van."

"You two plan to move her things alone?"

"We'll manage." She tilted her head to listen as the monitors came alive with the sound of Lynnie's cries. "Your daughter's awake."

"What time did you tell Granny you'd be there?"

"Ten thirty."

"I'll help. Granny Marie can't move her things."

Diedra stopped searching for her shoe and looked up at him. A smile trembled on her lips, and Eli rewarded her with one of his own. "Do you think you should?" she asked. "Lynnie's been so sick."

"Lynnie can stay with her at your place while we pick up her belongings."

"I'll call Granny in the morning and fill her in on the plan." She looked at him. "You're sure you want to help?"

"I'm not totally against her moving in," Eli said. "Truthfully, I can't say what bothers me."

"I can't bear to see her miserable. Besides, she's afraid she's going to become a cause of disagreement in her son's marriage. I have room and can use the company. That's why I offered."

He folded her close. "I know I don't understand, but I'm trying."

Diedra lifted her hand and wiped away the tears then giggled. "You're good for me."

"I think we're good for each other."

She could only nod her agreement as he kissed her fingers before she left.

❧

"Eli is so kind," Granny said when Diedra outlined the plan to her on the phone the following morning. "Between him and Jimmy, my move should be no problem."

"Jimmy's helping?"

"My son admits he's smothered me since the accident. He promised he'd try to stop but not stop loving me. I told him I reckoned I could live with that," Granny added with a soft chuckle. "He wants me to make Thursday my weekly night for dinner and to spend every Sunday afternoon with him and the grandchildren. I'm pleased he's handling it so well."

"How's Francie taking the news?"

"Who knows? She keeps to herself. I doubt that she minds I'm leaving."

"I'm sure she does. I have to go, Granny," Diedra said, quickly ending the conversation when she heard Eli calling her name. "Eli will pick you up around ten thirty. We'll go back for your things. Make sure you show him where everything is. Bye."

Diedra dashed out of her office to find Eli on his way upstairs with his daughter. When they got to the second floor, she reached for Lynnie, smiling at him when he relinquished his hold.

"Granny said Jimmy's going to help. She also said he's making plans for Thursday night and Sunday afternoon visits. Get moving. I'll have breakfast ready when you get back."

"But I'm starving," he protested.

"Hurry back."

She watched him go down the steps, her face breaking into a wide smile when he stopped to blow her a kiss. She had to tell him the truth soon. Otherwise she had no right to tell him she loved him.

Downstairs Diedra found Gina setting up for the day. "Hi, sweetie," Gina cooed to the baby. "She takes my breath away."

"She is gorgeous," Diedra agreed. Eli and Kelly had certainly created a perfect child.

What would their children have looked like? The vision of a blue-eyed, blond-haired baby filled her head and teased Diedra with its elusiveness. She pushed the image away.

"You were miles away," Gina said. "I asked why Lynnie's here."

"Eli's helping Granny move."

"He must be wild about you." At Diedra's curious look, Gina added, "Not too many people volunteered to help her move."

Diedra felt her cheeks grow warm under Gina's scrutiny. "Okay. Eli and I have been seeing each other."

Gina smiled. "I'm glad. There's something about the two of you. It's as if you both know exactly what the other one—" She stopped. "Oh, you're good for each other."

"He's a wonderful man."

"I detected an interest when he started making those daily trips by your office."

"So you told me."

Gina shrugged, lifting her hands in mock helplessness. "What can I say? I'm a romantic."

❧

In the kitchen Diedra placed Lynnie in a high chair and gave her some banana slices to occupy her while she searched the refrigerator. Maybe she could convince Eli to stay for dinner. It would give him and Granny an opportunity to get better acquainted.

She cooked bacon in the microwave and placed it on a paper towel to drain while she cut up fresh fruit. Soon she had everything ready. Where were they? Maybe she should call. She picked up the phone as Granny pushed the kitchen door open.

"Good morning, Dee," she called, lingering to speak to Lynnie before coming over to hug her friend. "Eli's parking. It didn't make sense to waste a trip, so Jimmy helped him load some of the smaller boxes. I'll show him where they go."

"I promised Eli breakfast when he got back." Diedra ripped off a paper towel and dried her hands as she edged toward the back door. "I'll get him."

She stepped outside. He'd parked in the driveway and had the van door open. "Eli?"

"Look at these boxes!" he exclaimed. "And at least fifteen or twenty more are still at the house. Then there's the furniture."

She understood his surprise when she saw what they'd piled in the van on one trip. "Leave them for now. Breakfast is ready."

Eli drew her into his arms. She heard a knock on the center's window and turned to find a child standing there watching her. Diedra waved at the little girl then saw her giggle when Gina led her away from the window.

"Peeping Tom?" he asked.

She smiled. "Thomasina."

Eli laughed. "You live in a fishbowl. How am I supposed to tell you good morning?"

"Are you giving up so easily?" Diedra asked, her eyes twinkling.

"Never." He kissed her gently.

"Breakfast is ready. If I'd known Granny would change the plan, I'd have fed you before you left."

"I have a feeling Granny's going to change more than one of our plans." Eli smiled as he looped his arm around her waist.

By six o'clock Granny had settled in her new room. In between caring for Lynnie and preparing their evening meal, she had also unpacked a number of boxes.

"She's amazing," Eli whispered to Diedra when Granny insisted they stay put while she brought in the dessert. "When did she have time to cook?"

"She works rings around most people I know," Diedra told him. "I'm gasping for air when I try to keep up."

Granny set a chocolate chip pie topped with whipped cream before them. Eli inhaled his portion. "I can see why Diedra wants you for a roommate. That's the best food I've eaten in some time."

"What?" Diedra demanded playfully.

"Best food I've eaten since this morning," he amended.

"Oh, go on, Eli," Granny said. "Dee knows I'm a better cook. I taught her everything she knows."

Diedra laughed.

"Didn't you want to show Eli that new lighting system in the tunnel slide? After I do these dishes, Lynnie and I are going upstairs to watch our favorite program." She winked at Diedra and began stacking plates.

"Granny, don't. You're tired," Eli said, surprising Diedra with his concern.

"You did all the heavy work."

"We'll do the dishes later." He looked at Diedra, and she nodded.

Granny patted his shoulder. "Thanks for your help today. This old woman won't forget your kindness."

After she had gone, Eli and Diedra pulled on their jackets and stepped into the backyard.

"I see you're calling her Granny now."

"She asked me to today," Eli said.

He grew quiet as he scanned the well-kept fenced area. "You were lucky to find this much space."

"My grandparents lived here. I wish you could have met them."

"Tell me," he invited, taking her hand in his as they walked around the playground.

Diedra settled in a swing, smiling up at Eli when he gave her a push. "They were there for me when I needed them most," she whispered, the words almost lost in the wind that stirred the leaves on the trees. "They never looked for me to be different, and I loved them for that."

"What about your parents?"

She tensed. "Let's not talk about them."

Eli's hand covered Diedra's on the chain for a moment before he took the swing next to hers. Idly he pushed himself about with his foot.

"Moving takes a lot out of you." He sighed. "Jimmy's an okay guy. He seemed to be taking it pretty well. He told me the whole mess was his fault. He feels he didn't check on his mother often enough. He mentioned the accident and indicated he felt guilty about it."

She was thankful he'd changed the subject. "Granny fell and broke her hip. They didn't find her until the next day. After they operated, she stayed in the hospital for a while then went to a rehab facility for therapy. She doesn't blame him. She's just trying to get her life back."

"Maybe it's working."

"I hope so. That's her biggest concern. She doesn't want to alienate her family, but she wants to go home."

Eli twisted the swing to one side and looked at her. "That Francie's a different one. I thought she'd breathe fire for a minute when Granny pointed out the furniture pieces she planned to take."

Diedra found his comment puzzling.

"I suspect Francie's coveted them for a while, and when Granny moved in they became feature attractions in her decorating scheme."

Diedra shook her head. "I'd love to give her a piece of my mind."

"Not too much, I hope."

"Very funny," Diedra said.

"What did you have to show me?"

"You're not too bright if you can't see past that old matchmaker's way of encouraging us to spend time alone."

He laughed. "So I have support in the camp?"

"As if you need it," Diedra murmured.

eleven

"I don't like the idea of your spending Thanksgiving alone," Granny repeated for the third time.

Diedra almost screamed when the subject came up again. Why was her lack of plans for the holiday causing so much concern? She retrieved the bread basket from the counter and offered Eli one of Granny's freshly baked yeast rolls. His eyes sparkled as he folded back the cloth and took out a roll.

"You're going to Jimmy's," she told Granny. "You convinced me to indulge myself in a mini-vacation. I have these fantastic plans in which I do absolutely nothing all day."

"But you'll be alone," Granny objected. "At least come for dinner."

"No," Diedra said firmly. "Jimmy and Francie's guest list is full. You go and have a good time with your family. I'm going to the nursing home in the afternoon anyway."

"I'll go with you," Granny said stubbornly.

"Please don't make a big deal of this, Granny," Diedra said.

"It doesn't make sense to me," the older woman grumbled. "Why would anyone want to spend Thanksgiving alone?"

Diedra turned her attention to her supper.

❧

While Granny was talking, Eli studied Diedra. He knew without asking that she wasn't going home for the holiday. He charged in, unsure how Diedra would react. "She won't be alone on Thanksgiving, Granny."

Both women stared at him. "I'm taking her to my house to

taste the wonderful things I do with dressing. I'd tell you, but it's a secret family recipe."

A smile wreathed Granny's face. "I'm so glad. I can enjoy myself knowing neither of you will be alone."

His gaze lingered on Diedra's face. "Having her there will make a world of difference. It's Lynnie's first Thanksgiving," he said when Diedra started to object.

"Lynnie couldn't care less about the holiday," Diedra pointed out.

"You know how important family traditions are," Eli said with a grin. "Maybe we'll test the new food processor I bought. The salesperson told me I could make my own baby food. I wonder how Lynnie would like homemade turkey and dressing with a hint of cranberry sauce."

"You don't want to upset her stomach," Granny warned.

"Just joking. Her turkey and peas will come in a jar."

After dinner Granny took Lynnie upstairs while Diedra and Eli started on the dishes. She played with the suds that frothed in the sink. "Why did you tell Granny I'm spending Thursday with you?"

Thursday, Eli thought. *Not Thanksgiving. Even earlier she referred to it as a holiday, but not Thanksgiving.* "Because you are."

Frowning, she slid the plates into the sink, splashing water onto the counter. "When did I ask you to make plans for me?" she asked huffily.

"Give me one good reason why you won't come," Eli said, ignoring her angry question. He tossed the drying towel on the countertop and grabbed her soapy hands from the water, holding them tightly. "Please do me the honor of spending Thanksgiving with us. It's a difficult time for me. Mom, Dad, and Kelly always made a big deal of holidays. I never spent a family holiday without being with family."

"You have Lynnie."

"As you said, she doesn't understand what Thanksgiving means. I want you there. Please say you'll come."

"Oh, okay. But I have to go to the nursing home in the afternoon. I always take flowers to those without families."

His eyes brimmed with tenderness. "It's a deal."

He dropped her hands, and she resumed washing the plates. "Tell me about the McKay family traditions."

Eli dabbed at his wet shirt with the drying cloth and proceeded to tell her how his family gave thanks.

❧

Thursday dawned overcast and dreary, and Diedra lay in bed considering the plans they had made. Eli would bring the brightness into her day. He would make her laugh and remind her of the things for which she should thank God. She threw back the covers.

He arrived early so they could go over to his church to package and deliver plates of food to shut-ins. They returned home shortly after eleven, just as Jimmy and Granny were leaving. After waving good-bye, they placed Lynnie in the playpen and began to transfer the cut flowers from the house.

"It looks like a flower garden out there," Eli said when he returned for another load. He lifted one of the remaining two boxes and tried to still the clatter of glass vases.

"This is it," Diedra said, taking the box of bows.

"There's another one over there."

"Granny's contribution to our dinner," Diedra said. "Sweet potato casserole and your favorite pie."

"Okay!"

Diedra laughed when he set the box of vases down and took the food first.

At his house Eli parked in the garage and began unloading boxes while Diedra removed Lynnie from her seat.

Eli lifted the two buckets of fresh-cut flowers she had purchased. "Why not have the florist deliver them?"

"I enjoy making them for each person."

"To brighten otherwise lonely lives. You're one special lady."

"Glad you think so," she murmured.

After she settled Lynnie in the nursery, Diedra found Eli watching the parade on a small television mounted under the kitchen cabinets.

"That isn't getting our dinner cooked."

Eli snared her hand, pulling her closer and resting his chin on her shoulder. His arms about her waist secured her into place. Diedra started giggling when he burst into song about loving parades. By the time he'd finished his emphatic rendition of the tune, her sides ached with laughter.

"I'd never have guessed," Diedra said as she watched the floats roll by the television cameras. Several minutes later she broke away and examined the items on the center island. She removed a peeler from the drawer and started working on the potatoes.

"I bought a turkey breast," Eli said as he stood and walked over to the oven door. "They don't make small birds."

"Maybe the growers think holidays are for big families," Diedra suggested.

"Only because they haven't realized there's something to be said for twosomes," he said, lifting his brows.

Diedra grinned. She finished peeling the potatoes and filled the bowl with cold water. "I'll go set the table."

"Do that. And make it cozy. I want my hostess beside me."

In the dining room Diedra reached for the fall centerpiece on the table and stopped when she read her name on a card tucked among the flowers. Her trembling fingers snapped open the sealed envelope. "With love on our first Thanksgiving."

Love. His thoughtful gifts always surprised her. Would they share another day like today? A Christmas? She had to tell him.

Diedra opened the antique buffet drawer and removed beautiful gold linen and hand-crocheted white tablecloths. After smoothing them over the table, she laid out the china and heirloom silver, all the while thinking of the McKay family traditions Eli had told her about.

Every family had them. At exactly seven o'clock on Thanksgiving Day, her parents sat down to their goose, never turkey. The twelve places at the Wynne table seated people who wouldn't dare refuse a Wynne family invitation.

As a child she had made an appearance before going to the kitchen to eat her meal with the staff. The years passed, and she joined the group at the dinner table; when she married, her parents welcomed Benjamin without reservation. Diedra shook her head as Benjamin intruded. Enough of that.

One final adjustment to the table linen, and she made another decision. Diedra hurried to the nursery and looked through Lynnie's closet. She pulled out the baby's prettiest dress—pale pink with a lacy froth of ruffles flowing from its waist. She located matching lace-trimmed socks and tiny black patent leather shoes. Perfect.

ॐ

"Diedra?" Eli called from the hallway. "Where are you?"

"In here."

He found her in Lynnie's room laying out clothes for the baby. "She'll look beautiful." He glanced down at his jeans and flannel shirt. "Something wrong with these?"

"We're dining formally," Diedra said as she tucked the

baby's socks into her shoes.

"And you?" Eli asked, his gaze lingering on her jeans and sweater.

"I'm going home to change into another outfit. You said you always dressed for dinner. Do you have a camera? I can bring mine so we can get a picture of you and Lynnie for the family album."

Her words brought back bittersweet memories of the arguments with his mother when she insisted they dress for dinner. Not that he or his dad ever won. But their time together always ended up being warm and inviting, a time of love. Eli wished they were here to meet Diedra.

"But we'll have to change before we go out again," Eli argued good-naturedly.

"A well-dressed group will never be turned away from anywhere."

"You won't be gone long, will you?"

She smiled. "No, I already know what I want. I can be back in thirty minutes."

"Okay," he agreed reluctantly. "Should I do anything else while you're gone?"

"We'll be eating at three. So you can work on dinner and have a sandwich to tide you over. If that doesn't keep you busy, start thinking about flower arrangements."

"Yes, ma'am, General Pierce!" Eli said, snapping his sneakers together and saluting her.

As Diedra started down the hallway, Eli dangled the car keys from his finger. "You'll need these."

❧

Later that afternoon they drove to the nursing home. Diedra considered Eli very handsome in his black suit. She wore a tobacco brown suit with a leaf-print blouse. All three of them brought smiles to a number of faces as they distributed flowers and visited with each person.

"How much longer?" Eli whispered. Lynnie had fallen asleep, and the flower supply on the cart had dwindled to three.

"We're finished. Those are for the nursing stations. Tired?"

"Sort of. It's been a busy Thanksgiving."

"Ready to get home to your game?"

"And a snack."

Diedra winked. "I think there's a sliver of pie left."

At the house Diedra changed Lynnie into a sleeper then went to the kitchen to make a snack.

In the sunroom Eli relaxed on the sofa. Diedra slid the tray of food onto the coffee table and smiled at him. "You look comfortable."

He pulled her down to sit on the sofa next to him then reached for a sandwich with his free hand. "Like football?"

"I never watch the game," Diedra admitted.

Eli spent several minutes explaining the plays. The conversation trailed off, and Diedra observed him while he watched the game. She smiled when he alternately cheered for and criticized the players, coaches, and referees.

At halftime Eli turned to Diedra. "When did you start visiting nursing homes?"

"My grandparents took me the first Thanksgiving I spent with them. Initially I didn't want to go. I couldn't imagine what I had in common with strangers until an elderly man shook my hand and told me how privileged he was to have met me. I understood then how important it was to them, and now I go whenever I can find the time."

"How can you be so selfless?"

"I get a lot of joy out of making them happy."

"I knew that. You always get joy from doing for others."

&

Eli held her hand as he thought of how little he'd given in his lifetime. Once he'd visited the children's ward at the hospital. He'd injured himself in a crash; his doctor suggested he might be able to brighten the spirits of a few of the long-term patients who were also race fans. He'd given his share of charitable contributions, but that hadn't been as rewarding as giving of himself today. Besides, if it made Diedra happy, he'd invite the entire retirement home to Christmas dinner. "Dee?"

"Yes?" She looked at him through blinking eyelids.

"Sorry. You're tired."

"Just lazy," Diedra said. "I always get that way when I'm full and content."

"You have tomorrow off. What do you say to driving to the mountains for the day to pick out Christmas trees?"

"That's a long ride for a tree."

"Not just trees. I promise you some of the best panoramic views you've ever seen. Plus some old family friends live up there, and we could visit them. What do you think?" Eli breathed in the faint floral scent of her perfume.

"Oh, why not?" she said finally. "What will we do with the turkey?"

"Make sandwiches?"

&

Eli drove up the next morning in a borrowed SUV. "We need it for the trees," he said, indicating the luggage rack on top.

They were on their way by seven thirty, stopped at a drive-through for breakfast, then headed for the mountains.

The radio played softly, and conversation came and went as they traveled the miles. Eli took the scenic route, and Diedra enjoyed the views that seemed to go on forever. At times she could have stuck out her hand and touched the mountainside. "It's incredible."

"I want to bring you back next year in late September, early October," Eli said. "There's something spectacular about majestic mountains with a backdrop of colorful trees—palettes of orange, rust, red, gold, and green. We can even do the tourist things if you want."

Diedra recalled memories from her childhood. She'd been ten or so when her grandparents brought her to the mountains. She had memories of Tweetsie Railroad and the train robbers, the elevator up through the mountains, and the chair lift at Maggie Valley. "What did you plan for today?"

"Nothing strenuous. I talked to the Kings after you left last night, and they insisted we come for lunch. After that we'll visit the tree farm."

"Sounds wonderful," Diedra said.

"I thought you would appreciate it. We have Lynnie, but I don't think she'll be as demanding as a center full of kids."

"Compared to my usual number, she's a day in the park. I hope everything's okay at the center."

"No work talk allowed," Eli said, reaching for the radio as the hourly news came on. The reporter covered the world and daily news before mentioning a local murder trial. He highlighted the testimony of the victim's sister, who said the police had documented the husband's abuse numerous times.

Diedra's heart pounded. She could have been that victim, but she would have had no one to testify in her defense.

"I don't understand why women tolerate that," Eli said as he lowered the volume.

"Mostly because they don't feel they have a choice."

"But there's so much help," he said. "Family. The police. Domestic violence shelters."

"It's not always enough."

He grimaced. "I don't ever want to see Lynnie in that sort of situation. I'd probably kill the man with my bare hands."

"Then make sure she develops tons of self-confidence and tell her she should never take abuse from any man."

Aware of his gaze on her, Diedra grabbed her purse and pretended to look for something, finally settling on a roll of breath mints. She offered him one then carefully peeled away the paper to take the next mint for herself.

"I'm sure she'll be very confident, since I'm not letting her date until she's thirty," Eli said, chuckling.

Diedra's smile waned as she considered her own confidence level when she met Benjamin. A recent college graduate, she'd been ready to conquer the world. She couldn't remember when fear had taken over—maybe when she discovered no one believed her husband was capable of cruelty.

Overwhelming sadness filled her. Another right time and she hadn't told him. Knowing she hadn't trusted him enough to share the truth would probably infuriate Eli.

"Are you still with me?" he asked, turning onto the driveway that led to the Kings' home.

Diedra brought her thoughts back to the present. The past was not going to ruin their day. "Tell me about your friends."

"They're good people. They were my parents' friends." Eli pulled into a graveled area and parked the car. "I used to come up here often, but I haven't been for a long time. I couldn't make myself come."

"Why not?"

"My mom loved the mountains. We came here for three weeks every summer. That's how my parents met the Kings. They honeymooned in a cabin just down the road from their place."

Diedra slipped a hand over Eli's. "I'm sorry. I can understand why your mom loved this area. It's beautiful."

She opened the car door and stepped out. Diedra heard the rush of water nearby. "It sounds as if there's a stream."

Eli stood and stretched. "There isn't much to it right now, but come spring, when the snow melts, it overflows its banks."

Diedra admired the rustic log cabin. "What a beautiful home."

"Wait until you see inside."

Diedra unfastened Lynnie from her car seat and joined Eli as they walked toward the house. The door swung open, and an elderly couple stepped onto the wraparound porch.

"Eli," the woman said, smiling. "We're so glad you're here."

He hugged them both. "Mr. and Mrs. King, this is my friend Diedra Pierce." He reached for the baby. "And my daughter, Lynnie."

"We're so glad you could come," Mrs. King told Diedra before her gaze focused on the baby. "Oh, Tom, look at her. Your parents would be so proud, Eli."

Lynnie started to whimper.

"Time for a bottle," Eli said.

"Then come on in," Mr. King said. "Let's not keep the little lady waiting."

Within minutes Diedra sat holding the baby and watching as Lynnie's tiny bud of a mouth worked greedily to assuage her hunger.

She couldn't imagine a homier environment. The stone fireplace occupied one full wall, the crackling logs warding off the chill of the day. Comfortable leather furniture suited the area, as did the large Christmas tree that stood in the corner.

"Your home is beautiful," she told Mrs. King after accepting the cup of coffee. "I love your tree."

"Thank you. We decorated it last night." She smiled at her husband as she joined him on the sofa. "How did you and Eli meet?"

"Lynnie comes to my day care center."

"I could tell she's very comfortable with you," Mrs. King said. "So, Eli, tell us what's been going on with you."

"Lynnie keeps me busy."

"How's your work?" Mr. King asked.

"Doing well." Eli sipped his coffee and set the mug back on the wooden coffee table. "It's been hectic this year. It's good to get away for a day."

"You have a standing invitation to visit anytime you like," the older man said.

"I miss coming up here. Seeing the area today brought back so many good memories."

The conversation drifted into the past years, and Diedra enjoyed hearing about Eli's escapades as a young boy. "He was a handful," Mrs. King told Diedra. "His parents never knew what he'd do next." She glanced at Eli. "Do you remember the time you jumped off the side of the barn?"

"Don't remind me. I wore that cast for eight weeks."

A timer buzzed in the kitchen. "Lunch is ready," Mrs. King said. "Hope you don't mind turkey pot pie."

"Not at all." Diedra glanced at Eli and smiled. "We had the same dilemma with leftover turkey yesterday. We have sandwiches in a cooler in the car."

"I prefer turkey pot pie any day," Eli said.

The meal consisted of a combination of Thanksgiving leftovers along with the hot dish and a salad.

"You're a wonderful cook," Diedra said after finishing the last bite of her slice of red velvet cake. "I need exercise."

"I promised Dee a walk along your trails," Eli said.

"Good idea. Why don't you leave Lynnie here with us? Let her finish her nap."

Eli glanced at Diedra.

"We'll help you clean up first," Diedra said.

"Nonsense. I'm going to load all this into the dishwasher."

"I'll get my coat from the car."

They headed into the woods, following the trail that led up to a roaring waterfall. Diedra stopped at every turn to gaze at the beautiful scenery. She enjoyed the peace and quiet most of all. The wind rustled in the trees and leaves. The same leaves crunched underneath their feet, until they spotted some wildlife and tried to be still. It didn't take long for the deer to catch their scent and dart away.

Eli wrapped an arm around her shoulders, and they continued to walk in comfortable silence. After a while he glanced at his watch. "We'd better head back. Time to buy the Christmas trees."

The Kings directed them to their favorite tree farm, and after a flurry of hugs and good-byes, they were soon on their way.

They found the tree farm easily and spent the next couple of hours searching for the perfect tree. Every time they thought they'd found one, another more just-right tree caught their attention.

"This is it," Diedra said, pointing to the tree she wanted.

"Isn't this the first one you liked so much?" Eli asked.

Diedra giggled. "Probably. I think we've been wandering in circles for too long."

They selected the four trees they wanted and watched as the man felled each one, running them through a machine that secured them in netting.

She stood to the side with Lynnie as the men struggled to hoist them atop the SUV. Just when she decided it was an impossible task, Eli flashed her a happy grin and fastened the rope the man tossed over the top of the vehicle. "Didn't think we could do it, did you?"

"I never doubted you for a minute," she teased.

They stopped at a picnic area on the way home and found a table a short distance from the vehicle. Lynnie drained her bottle in record time and drifted off to sleep.

The view was breathtaking. "The fog looks like smoke over the mountains," Diedra said.

"Probably why they call them the Great Smoky Mountains."

Diedra tapped his arm playfully and spread out the sandwiches, chips, and veggies he'd packed in the cooler.

"Good sandwich," Eli said afterward, balling up the wrappers and tossing them into a nearby trash can.

Diedra nodded. "I didn't think I could eat another bite after that lunch Mrs. King served," Diedra told him.

"But all that walking and tree shopping gave you an appetite?"

"I suppose so. I've enjoyed myself today."

He took her hand in his. "Me, too. I hope we can do this again."

&

Diedra found herself almost too tired to sleep when Eli dropped her off at home later that night. She tossed and turned restlessly and finally dozed off. A nightmare woke her in the early hours of the morning. She pulled on her robe and went downstairs to make a cup of cocoa.

The dream lingered in her head, and she felt guilty. Yesterday had been wonderful. She couldn't remember a nicer holiday, and Eli deserved the credit. Most women spent their entire lives looking for Mr. Right, the perfect man. In her case she had fallen at his feet that first meeting.

Pity she couldn't return the favor for Eli. In her dream Diedra had revealed the truth to him, and he told her it was over. Not because of what she'd shared but because he hated deceit. Because she hadn't believed in him. Even thinking of the dream sent cold shivers down her spine.

She sat at the table and bowed her head. *Dear God, help me. I'm wrong to keep secrets from the man I love because I'm afraid. Give me the words to tell him what I should have from the beginning.*

twelve

As Diedra listened to the drone of the television, she realized loneliness had not been a factor in her life lately. Since she'd started dating Eli and Granny had moved in, at times she longed for a few minutes to herself.

Granny's presence left little time for her and Eli to be alone, but the older woman also made certain Diedra didn't stay locked in the confines of her decision not to become involved again. She often babysat so they could go on dates.

Ever since their argument about Granny's move, Eli had kept his opinions on the subject to himself. When Diedra made excuses to stay home with Granny, his face revealed his disappointment, but he didn't say a word.

At first he'd picked up Lynnie from the day care center and gone home. Then after a few nights they drifted into a pattern of eating together. Eli usually refused at first but gave in to Granny's argument that he had to eat anyway. Afterward he would help with the dishes, and then they would join Granny in the upstairs sitting room.

Eli had even taken to attending church with them on Sundays. He placed Lynnie in the nursery then sat with them in the sanctuary.

His spiritual knowledge surprised Diedra more than once when Granny mentioned something from the sermon and Eli offered the view of a man who had read his Bible more than a few times.

Wanting things to be perfect for everyone placed Diedra in

an impossible situation. She justified her actions, telling herself she deserved happiness for just a little longer. But the guilt increased daily, and she knew she had to tell Eli the truth.

She snuggled under the chenille afghan and watched the Christmas tree lights twinkle. She was thankful her staff had decorated the big tree downstairs, and Eli's staff had taken care of the one at his business. They had decorated the one at his house Tuesday night, and Granny had helped with this one last night. Eli insisted on themes, and they combed through their combined decorations to come up with sufficient ideas to make the trees original.

Not only had they finished the trees, but they also had hung garland and wreaths and placed other Christmas mementos around the living room. Eli's favorite was an old mechanical figure that had belonged to Diedra's grandfather. He was like a child crying, "Do it again," when she showed him how it worked.

She'd enjoyed herself immensely until the conversation shifted to families.

"Have you finished your shopping?" Granny asked as she picked up the tangled lights Eli had tossed down in despair.

Eli shook his head. "Who has time?" The lights flashed on as he tested the last bulb in another strand.

"Not me," Diedra agreed.

"Funny how certain things become less important as you get older," Eli said. "A few years ago I'd never have dreamed I'd be comfortable with having no plans for every evening of the week. You learn family's more important than good times."

Diedra couldn't hold back the grief that overwhelmed her every time she thought about the natural progression of the conversation. A suffocating sensation tightened her throat, and she pushed up the barriers that shut everyone out when it came her time to share.

Transported back in time, Diedra sat before her father's desk, trying to make him understand she needed his help.

"Things like this don't happen to women in your social status," James Wynne argued. "Do you have any idea how these lies will hurt Benjamin's reputation? No respectable firm would tolerate the bad publicity."

"I'm not lying, Daddy!" she had cried out.

"Go home, Diedra. You're a lucky woman to have such a successful husband."

Shame had kept her from confiding in others. She had no friends. Benjamin had long since made sure of that. The people they associated with as a couple would have listened only to gossip about the sordid details.

Given Benjamin's legal background, Diedra convinced herself the police would never believe her over him. Alone in her struggle, she feared the monster she'd married.

Two men had hurt her: the husband who abused, ridiculed, and made her feel worthless and the father who scolded and treated her like a little girl. At least she understood her father's reasoning.

Publicity had always been her parents' greatest horror. Nothing could defile the Wynne family name, the family honor, but in the end Diedra won.

"Mother expects to inherit the house," Diedra had protested when her grandparents told her their plans.

"Elizabeth sees this house only as prime real estate. She doesn't need it the way you do," her grandfather said. "It's our choice, Dee. Make two old people happy."

After weeks of agonizing she realized she had no choice but to agree. Diedra watched as both signed over their home to her in their lawyer's office. Before their deaths her grandparents spent a great deal of time helping her make and carry out plans for the center.

Elizabeth Wynne attended her mother's funeral then waited for the lawyer to read the will. She accused Diedra of turning her parents against her then refused to listen to any reply and returned to California. They had not spoken since.

Sometimes fear of becoming like her parents gnawed at Diedra, and she wished she were the child of more loving and forgiving parents. Diedra knew her mother had never been content with her lot in life and that she couldn't wait to get away from her parents' strict upbringing and do things her way.

James Wynne's money allowed her mother to live the life she coveted, and soon a wide chasm spread between her mother and her grandparents. Diedra suspected her mother sometimes felt guilt over the way she treated them but eased her conscience by sending them expensive gifts. Diedra had witnessed their sadness when their daughter didn't visit.

The door chimes echoed throughout the house. Diedra threw the afghan aside and fumbled for her bedroom shoes.

"I'm coming," she called when the chimes started up again the moment her foot touched the varnished floorboards of the hallway.

One glance through the side window, and she opened the door quickly.

"Eli? Janice said you were working."

Diedra had offered to keep Lynnie earlier when he called to tell her Janice would pick up the baby. At first she'd been offended, but after giving the matter more consideration, she realized Eli was giving her a break.

"I have been. Sort of," he admitted with a sheepish grin.

"If you came for supper, Granny's out."

He looked relieved. "Good. Honestly, Dee—I've got to skip some of those meals of hers or buy new clothes."

"I've gained five pounds since she moved in."

"I bought you something," he said, placing a small box in her hand.

She untied the ribbon and opened the box to reveal four of her favorite chocolates. Surprised, Diedra looked at him. "How did you know?"

"I asked Granny."

"You make me feel so special."

"You sound as if no one ever did anything special for you."

Diedra chewed her lower lip and stole a look at him.

"Why can't you tell me about your past, Dee?"

She knew her inability to share this with him bothered Eli. A mute appeal touched Diedra's face. "Please don't spoil my evening."

"I want to get to know you."

Trapped in her own lie, Diedra knew Eli could never know the person she had been. He would never respect that woman.

Eli hugged her close, and some of the tension drained from her. He couldn't understand her feelings. Sometimes even she couldn't. She wanted to love her parents again. She did love them. She simply didn't trust them.

Eli released her. "I meant it when I said I want to know you, Dee. Show me what you looked like as a little girl. Tell me your favorite things. What was your best friend's name? What kind of grades did you make? What are your hopes and dreams?"

Diedra's misgivings increased with each word. She didn't want to remember Diedra Wynne. And she'd spent years trying to forget when she was Mrs. Benjamin Pierce. In her haste to change the subject, Diedra fumbled with the little box. "Time for dessert."

The amaretto filling of the chocolate candy oozed over her fingers as Diedra took a bite then gave him the remainder.

She sighed. "Hmm. Addictive."

"I couldn't concentrate tonight," he said. "I need to talk to you."

She looked at him curiously. "About what?"

He seemed very uncomfortable.

"I care a great deal about you, and I think you care for me as well."

"You know I do. What's wrong, Eli?" Was he experiencing doubts?

He looked at her. "Today is the first anniversary of Kelly's death. It's been difficult. I keep thinking about her."

"We don't forget those we love. We just pick up and go on with our lives because that's expected of us."

Eli studied her. "You understand. You lost your husband."

Her relationship with Benjamin had never resembled Eli's marriage. She pushed the thought away and considered what she could say to comfort him. The usual things—how it gets easier with time, with each passing year. She paused as the thought struck her. "You said Kelly's been dead a year. How can that be? Lynnie's only ten months old."

"Can we go into your office? There's something I feel you should know."

Diedra's eyes closed. *Not another man with a secret. Please, God, not Eli, too.* She had already loved one man who had hidden something terrible. Her apprehension grew at his solemn expression.

She led the way and sat in one of the blue leather chairs. Eli sat in the other one.

"Lynnie is our biological child," he began, obviously ill at ease. "But a surrogate brought our baby into the world."

Her eyes widened in astonishment. "A surrogate?"

"Yes," he said. "My wife wasn't able to carry a child, so the doctor took our biological child—our fertilized egg—and implanted it into another woman who carried it on our behalf."

His revelation threw her thought processes into a tailspin. "You paid someone to give birth to your child? Why, Eli?" she asked when he nodded.

"Did you ever watch someone grieving to death?"

Diedra thought of the times she'd done exactly that. She'd focused on what she'd lost instead of thanking God for what she'd gained.

"After she lost our second baby, Kelly slipped into a deep depression. She cried all the time. She barely ate. I watched her waste away. It killed me to have her want a child so badly. I suggested adoption, but she wouldn't consider that. She insisted I needed a son to carry on the family name.

"I argued that a child of the heart would serve the same purpose, but she wouldn't listen. This went on for months. She consulted doctors. She read everything she could find on the subject. Our marriage stopped being about us and became about having children. She was miserable. I was miserable.

"Then she told me she wanted a divorce. She'd decided that if she couldn't give me children, she would free me to find someone who could. I told her she was being ridiculous. That having a child wasn't that important."

Diedra gasped.

"Not very understanding, I know," he admitted. "But I was at the end of my rope. I refused to consider divorce. I told her I would never marry again if she left me, and she would be hurting us both unnecessarily. Things settled down for a while after that. Then she came up with the surrogate idea. She said we could have a biological child with another woman's help.

"Surrogacy was one of those things other people tried. But the more Kelly talked, the more I realized I couldn't come up with one reason to say no. Our decision wouldn't hurt anyone. The young woman liked being a surrogate. I weighed losing my wife against surrogacy and decided losing Kelly would be far worse. In the end it all came down to making Kelly happy."

"And was she happy?" Diedra asked.

"Ecstatic. Once our surrogate let us know we were expecting, Kelly was thrilled. She started planning the nursery right away. While I raced cars, she planned. We never passed a baby store that she didn't have to go in. I knew my life was about to change in a big way when she brought up buying a house and settling down.

"She'd stuck with me through the good and bad, so I knew it was my turn to show her support."

Diedra struggled with his revelation. She wanted to understand. "It never bothered you?"

"I think we blocked the reality and lived in the fantasy," Eli told her. "A couple of months after Lynnie was on the way, God began to work in our lives. We attended the funeral of a dear friend, and the message moved us both to repent that same day. Reality hit us hard, and we questioned whether we'd done the right thing."

"Lots of people make bad decisions before becoming Christians."

"I won't believe Lynnie is a mistake," Eli said.

"That's not what I meant," Diedra said. "I believe God knows the paths our lives will take. I believe that path often leads us to Him. I know I made more than one unguided choice of my own."

Eli took Diedra's hands in his. "Maybe so. But right or wrong, every time I see my wife in our child, I experience only joy. We joined a church and went to our pastor for counseling. He agreed we'd tampered in God's work, but he told us Jesus had paid the price for our sins and His grace would get us through.

"We couldn't undo what we'd already done. At that point we decided to raise our child in a godly home. A home filled with love. And then Kelly was killed by a speeding car."

Diedra understood his agony.

"God's strength was all that kept me going. That and the fact that I would be a father in a very short time. Kelly never got the opportunity to mother our child. The true irony is that despite her insistence I needed a male heir, we had a daughter. I've grieved for Kelly. I still do, but I have a responsibility to love and care for my child. I don't believe God makes mistakes. He brought Lynnie into this world as a healthy baby. And even when I have doubts, I can't take my eyes off God's promises. Lynnie is a precious gift. I don't know what the future holds, but I know God will be by my side. I want to prove myself worthy of the task He's set before me. I want to be the best father possible."

"You are one of the best I've ever known," Diedra said.

He squeezed her hand. "Do you want children, Diedra?"

She swallowed the lump in her throat. "I love children, and if possible I'd like a couple of my own."

Tell him the truth. Give him the chance to decide whether he wants to continue the relationship. Tell him.

"Eli—" Diedra began, desperation overcoming her at the thought of losing him. She couldn't. She watched the play of emotions on his face.

"You know what I think about? How Lynnie will feel when she learns the truth. Will she hate me for what we did?"

"Lynnie will ask questions. Your daughter loves you. There's no way she's going to stop."

"You stopped loving your parents," he pointed out.

Diedra's smile faded. "I love them. I need to forgive them for not supporting me at a time in my life when I needed them most."

"Oh, Dee," Eli said, drawing her to him.

She held on to Eli. How easily he and Lynnie had become part of her world. Her life would be miserable without them.

"Does knowing this make a difference to you?" he asked, tilting her face back to see her expression. "I understand you could find it morally offensive."

"Are you asking me to pass judgment on what you did?"

"People sometimes hold the circumstances of our birth against us," Eli said. "I couldn't bear it if the woman I cared for did that to my child."

Diedra stared at him. "I'd never do that to any child. Lynnie's a wonderful little girl. You're blessed to have her."

His relief was obvious. "Thank you. I didn't tell you this to pressure you into anything. You deserve to know before things go any further. Of course, I'm telling you this in the strictest confidence."

"I'd never share this with anyone," Diedra promised. She certainly knew how gossip could affect lives.

"I'd better go. It's getting late."

She followed Eli to the front porch. The enormity of what had just transpired hit Diedra like a ton of bricks. Eli trusted her with a secret. He trusted her with the truth, and she would never betray that trust.

God didn't make mistakes. Lynnie existed today because He intended her to be there. Diedra couldn't doubt that.

An even stronger realization hit her. Eli was serious about their relationship. He never would have told her this if he didn't have hopes for the future. Eli showed his love to her over and over again while she couldn't even say the words.

She loved him. But did she have the right?

Long after Eli had gone, Diedra agonized over what he'd told her. Knowing he and Kelly had wanted a child badly enough to go the surrogate route reinforced how impossible it was for her to commit to a future with Eli. He'd asked if she wanted kids. As much as he loved them, she knew he wanted more children. Why hadn't she told him the truth?

Diedra fully identified with Kelly—the agony she must have experienced at not being able to give birth to her own child. The agony Diedra suffered at the thought of never being able to do the same. Diedra clutched her arms around her waist, and the tears began to fall. It hurt. So much.

She wasn't being fair to Eli. "Oh, God, help me!" she cried, seeking comfort from the One who loved her even when she couldn't love herself.

thirteen

A night spent agonizing over Eli's truth didn't make things any better the next day. The weekend had been wonderful, but a knot formed in her stomach when Gina came back to work on Monday morning wearing a diamond. She'd turned in her resignation, explaining she wanted to move to Virginia Beach to be closer to her fiancé.

While happy for Gina, her friend as well as her favorite staff member, Diedra knew it would take her a long time to find someone who worked with the babies so well. Gina planned to stay long enough to train the new employee for the first two weeks. Of course, that depended on Diedra's choosing from among the many applicants.

"Thank you, Mrs. Adams." She checked the name on the application. "I'll be making my decision within the next week."

After the woman left, Diedra sighed and placed the most recent response to her employment ad in her in-basket.

As if Gina's leaving wasn't enough, two staff members succumbed to a stomach virus, and Diedra had to work in their classrooms. Long days with the children and evenings of decorating for Christmas exhausted Diedra. She'd hoped to get to bed early the previous evening, but Eli's news had left her tossing and turning through the night.

Granny had plans to stay with her grandchildren, and Janice had invited Diedra and Eli over for family night. Diedra had agreed earlier in the week, but with so much happening, she wished she could stay home. It was too late to change the plans now. Eli would pick her up at six thirty.

Diedra had just managed to shower and dress when the doorbell rang. She hurried downstairs and greeted Eli and Lynnie. Eli relinquished the baby to her, and Lynnie smiled and cooed at Diedra.

Eli's bright smile told her he was happy.

"She loves you," he said. "And I do, too."

Diedra's heart began to pound so hard she could scarcely breathe. "You what?"

"I said I love you."

Her gaze fixed on the collar of his sport shirt. "Eli?"

"Is that all you can say?" he teased. "It's not every day a man says he loves you, is it?"

Diedra swallowed hard and smiled faintly. "No, it isn't."

She didn't know what to do. One part of her wanted to return his love and forget the past. Another part argued that the past would always rear its ugly head to spoil the present and future.

How would Eli feel about the truth? She'd learned long ago that hers wasn't a pleasant story, and she had witnessed the changed attitudes of people who knew. Would he lose all respect for her? Could she handle it if he did?

"We'd better go, or we'll be late," she said, seeing his expression grow sad when she didn't return his sentiment.

Diedra handed Lynnie back to Eli and reached for her coat on the hall tree. He held it with his free hand as she slipped her arm inside.

At the car Eli strapped Lynnie into her car seat then slipped behind the wheel. He started the engine, hitting the heat control. "It's chilly out tonight."

Cold air shot out of the vents, and Diedra shivered.

"Sorry," he said, turning it off. "I thought it would still be warm from the drive over."

Diedra buttoned her coat and reached into the pockets for her gloves. "Cold weather is definitely not my favorite. I asked Janice if I could bring something, but she said no."

"I picked up a gift basket. She's excited that we're coming over," Eli said as he maneuvered into traffic.

"I really like Janice. I've met her husband a time or two when he picked up the children. He seems very nice."

"They make a great couple," Eli agreed.

A few minutes later he parked behind Janice's green van. The Gores welcomed them inside, and Davey whisked Diedra away to show her their Christmas decorations.

A magnificent live tree stood in the living room and another in the family room. Davey fell to his knees and turned on the train that was spread out under the tree. They spent a couple of minutes playing engineer before he dragged her to his room. A small tree decorated in cartoon characters sat in his window seat. Diedra admired the nativity scene on Davey's nightstand.

"The baby Jesus was born at Christmas," Davey told her, picking up each piece of the set to tell her about it. "Kaylie has a tree, too." He caught her hand and led her to his sister's bedroom where Diedra viewed yet another small tree.

"Everything is beautiful," she said to Janice, who had come to tell them the pizza had arrived. "When did you find time to put up four trees?"

"Don't tell anyone," Janice said, "but we store the little trees already decorated. Remove the bag and fluff them out—instant tree."

Diedra laughed. "Wish I could figure out how to do that with the bigger varieties. I threaten to buy one of those pre-lighted artificial trees every year, but I never do."

"Me, too. David insists the kids would be upset, but I know

who doesn't want an artificial tree. He goes on and on about the scent. Never mind the mess they make. Just so long as they smell good." They laughed together as they walked into the dining room.

"There you are," Eli called to Diedra. "I thought you'd gotten lost."

"Davey had lots to show me."

Janice smiled at that. "He loves Ms. Dee."

"I love him, too."

She sat beside Eli, and he leaned over and whispered, "I wouldn't mind hearing you say those words to me."

Davey dragged a chair over and placed it between them, and Eli said no more about it.

The conversation flowed as they ate pizza and drank soda. Eli told them about their day trip to the mountains, and Janice and David talked about their visits to both sets of grandparents.

Diedra helped Janice clean up while Eli and David took Lynnie and Kaylie into the family room. Janice put the leftover pizza into the other box and closed it. "I'm glad you came with Eli."

"I'm enjoying myself."

"I hope we can do this more often. I've never seen Eli so happy."

Diedra was suddenly struck by the feeling that Janice could soon see him miserable again. She didn't want her to be upset with her. "What if it doesn't work out?" Diedra asked finally.

"Do you think it won't?" Janice pulled out a chair and sat down. "Let's talk about it."

"I don't really see how we can make this work," Diedra said.

"You seem happy together."

Diedra wrung her hands in her lap, glad the wooden tabletop

hid her action. "I've been keeping things from Eli. Things I should have told him. I've fought my conscience for weeks. Then tonight he said he loved me. I've been so unfair to him."

"Don't you love him?"

"If only it were that simple. I care a great deal for Eli, but I find it very difficult to trust. I'm afraid."

"God didn't give us a sense of fear, Diedra."

"I know. Granny tells me the same thing. In my heart I know if my secrets hurt Eli, I've wronged him. How can I expect him to forgive me when I've let this go on far too long?"

"Why haven't you told him before?" Janice asked curiously.

"I've meant to. But every time an opportunity comes, fear strangles me, and I clam up. I've hinted at some things, but I haven't told him the truth."

"You need to open up to Eli. Tell him what you're holding back and take it from there. You can't say how he'll react until he knows. Because he loves you, I'd be willing to say he'll be able to deal with the truth."

"I'm such a coward."

Janice patted her hand. "Falling in love gives us a different perspective. We stop thinking of ourselves and consider how our behaviors affect others. You're definitely doing that. David and I learned early on that communication is key."

David stuck his head in the kitchen door and smiled. "Hey, what's keeping you two?"

"We'll be right there," Janice said then turned back to Diedra after he had left. "I'll pray for you. Trust God to give you strength to do what's right."

The men had already set up the game table. Lynnie crawled around the family room while Kaylie watched and clapped her hands. When Diedra sat down, Lynnie crawled over and pulled herself up against her legs.

"Well, aren't you a smart girl?" Diedra said, smiling when she lifted the baby into her lap.

"She's been doing that for a few days now," Eli said. "She's testing her sea legs holding on to the sofa and coffee table."

Diedra glanced at Janice. "I've been watching Kaylie in the nursery. I pray she takes her first steps at home."

Janice patted her hand. "Don't worry about it. Tell Gina to record the specifics. And give me a call, of course. I'll check on the video monitoring."

"Gina turned in her resignation this week. She's moving to Virginia Beach to marry her soldier."

"I'm happy for her," Janice said, "but sad for us. She's excellent with the kids. Are you giving her a bridal shower?"

"We should."

"Let me know how I can help."

"Are we going to play or talk weddings?" David asked and winked at his wife.

"Diedra and I will play you and Eli," Janice told her husband. "Prepare to lose."

And win they did. Diedra had never been good at games, but Janice made up the deficit.

"We give up!" Eli exclaimed when the women won the fifth game in a row.

"You don't want to defend your manhood?" Janice countered with a wide grin.

Eli glanced at his daughter, who was sleeping in Diedra's arms. "It's past Lynnie's bedtime."

Kaylie had fallen asleep on a cushion on the floor, and Davey scooted his toy cars around the room while a children's video played on the television.

"They'll have to defend it another time," Diedra said. "Tomorrow's a workday."

"You'll have to be my partner again," Janice told her, smiling. "I never win against these guys."

❧

Eli arrived on time the following morning. His lighthearted mood caused Diedra to wonder if admitting her feelings for him would help her feel the same kind of joy. Or was it the relief he felt after revealing the truth about Lynnie? "I guess I'd better go," he said after a few minutes of reminiscing about the previous night. "Take care of my baby girl."

"I always do. Have a good day."

Diedra helped in the classrooms and monitored the playground, and after lunch with the children, she settled at her desk with the applications for the teacher position. A week of Gina's notice time had already passed. She'd barely started reading when the phone rang.

"Hello, sweetheart."

"You should wait until you know who's on the phone," Diedra said.

"Why? The chance I'll get a sweetheart every time is a hundred percent."

"Maybe not this sweetheart."

"Then I have a problem, because you're the only one I want."

His words thrilled her. If things could be different, Diedra couldn't imagine anything better than Eli's love.

"I called to see what your plans for the afternoon are."

"Plans?" she asked. "The same as usual—work."

"Let's take the afternoon off. I have to do some Christmas shopping."

She glanced at the piles of paper on her desk. "I have interviews to arrange."

"Just say yes or no."

"And if I refuse?"

Eli sighed. "I suppose I could go alone. Oh, say yes. I'd like to see you."

Diedra wanted to see him, too. "When and where?"

"In one hour at the mall. I'll buy you a hot dog in the food court."

"You go ahead. I ate lunch with the kids today."

As she stepped into the busy mall an hour later, Diedra searched for Eli. She waved when she spotted him at a table across the room.

"Just in time," he said, kissing her cheek before grabbing his trash from the table.

He took her hand and outlined the gifts he planned to buy as they walked through the mall. The toy store was first on his list, and they spent the next hour picking out items suitable for Lynnie.

"I love toy stores. I want to buy out the place."

"Just remember how many times you'll have to pick up every toy you buy," Diedra said.

"That's a good argument for controlling my buying impulse."

"Good. Now I can buy more for her," Diedra said with a burst of laughter.

He arranged for the toy store to hold his bags while they continued shopping. They strolled through the mall, and when they arrived at a jewelry store, he led her inside. "I want to get something special for Granny."

Diedra followed as Eli moved from case to case.

"What about that?" he asked, pointing out an exquisite enameled brooch.

"I'm sure she'd love it."

He asked to see the brooch then examined it closely. "I'll take it."

"May I show you something for the lady?" the salesclerk asked with a smile.

Eli glanced at Diedra. "Yes, I think you can. We'd like to see your engagement rings."

Her breath caught in her chest, and she feared she would suffocate for lack of air. Eli started to follow the woman.

"Diedra?" he called when she didn't move. Eli reached to touch the blond curl that nestled against her cheek.

"Eli, no," she managed finally.

"It's time, Diedra. Marry me?"

Her shocked teal eyes gazed into his silver-blue eyes. Frozen in limbo, a place where all decisions and actions were impossible, Diedra knew the time had come. The time when secrets were going to take from her everything she needed for survival.

Eli grasped her hand. "Marry me, Diedra. Help me give Lynnie the family she needs."

Her eyelids fluttered downward in an attempt to mask the fear. "I can't, Eli. I'll love you always, but I can't marry you."

"Why not?" His brows furrowed.

Diedra glanced at the clerk, and Eli told her he'd come back for the brooch. He led Diedra out into the mall toward the seating area.

The silence lengthened, making her uncomfortable. All along Diedra had been careful not to say things to destroy his illusions about her, truths that would make him think her weak. She could keep her precious control and never lose his respect. But she couldn't respect herself if she did that to Eli.

"I do love you, Eli." Diedra's voice cracked as tears trailed down her face. "I just can't let you tie yourself to a barren woman."

She turned and ran, weaving in and out of shoppers, looking for a place to hide.

"Diedra, wait!" Eli called. "Sweetheart, please."

She slipped out of a side exit and prayed he wouldn't follow.

ও

Stunned, Eli moved faster than he would have believed possible. He searched the crowds. Where had she gone? A sense of inadequacy swept over him. This was his fault. He hadn't encouraged her enough to talk about her past.

ও

Diedra didn't feel relief when she reached her car and climbed inside. An angry woman stared back at her in the rearview mirror. "Why?" Her tortured cry rose with the pain that ripped through her. She'd had so many opportunities to tell Eli the truth. "Whatever made you believe you could get beyond your problems? Your self-doubts?"

She fumbled the key into the ignition and started the engine then backed out of the parking space. The blare of a horn forced her to slam on the brakes, rocking the car with the sudden stop. She pulled back into the space and rested her head on the steering wheel, her chest tightening so much she could hardly breathe.

The thought of losing Eli shattered her, but she couldn't gain her own happiness at his expense. It wouldn't work. In time he'd blame her, and she'd lose him, too.

Be fair to him, she told herself, biting her lip until it throbbed. *He deserves the best, and that's not you.* Diedra covered her face with trembling hands. *It'll never be you.* What had she done to deserve this? A stab of guilt penetrated her thoughts. What had Eli done?

He'd loved her. But she'd kept secrets. And secrets destroyed. Her teeth chattered when a chill as freezing as an arctic blast pervaded her soul. Where could she go? Not home. Eli would find her there.

❧

"You don't know where she is?" Eli asked again. He hadn't been able to think clearly since Diedra had disappeared in the mall.

Upstairs in the apartment, Granny sat in an armchair, her hands clasped tightly in her lap. "I don't know. I haven't heard from her since she left around two this afternoon. Eli, what happened?"

His hand swept over his face. "We were Christmas shopping." He hesitated. "I–I asked her to marry me. She said no." His neck throbbed from the tension knotted there; his stomach churned. "Where does she go to be alone?"

"This place is her refuge."

"And she won't come home because of me," he said, sinking into a nearby chair. "Oh, Granny, what have I done?"

"Nothing that wouldn't have happened sooner or later. You've forced her to confront the truth." Granny reached over and patted his hand.

"What truth? I thought we were heading in the right direction. Everything just blew up. I don't understand."

Granny looked concerned. "She didn't tell you why?"

"She threw out something about not wanting to tie me to a barren woman. What did she mean? Does it have to do with her rift with her family? Her marriage?"

Granny looked hopeful. "She told you?"

"She's tried to share some things. Vague comments about her parents and trust issues she has. I knew she was holding something back, but I figured I could wait until she was ready to tell me. I should have realized she was crying out for help. Instead, I selfishly took everything she had to give for myself."

"Eli, don't blame yourself. She's a giver. Diedra looks out for everyone but herself, but she'll have to do that now. She won't allow anyone else to help."

"You know something you're not telling," Eli said, shifting forward in the seat.

Granny nodded slowly. "She's been hurt, but not by you. I suspect she feels she's protecting herself. She's wary, afraid to trust another human being with her love. And rightfully so. She's been subjected to so much pain and misery, but I know she will overcome it."

"How do you know?"

"Dee loves you, but she loves God more. He won't let her destroy herself."

Yes. God was in control. Eli closed his eyes and opened his heart in prayer, thanking His Savior for the grace He gave him every day. He pleaded for God to provide Diedra a safe harbor and comfort during this time of tempest.

fourteen

Diedra closed the motel door and shoved the lock in place. The room had seen better days. The mattresses on both double beds had noticeable sags in the middle, and the scarred furnishings belonged to the fifties. She didn't care. Here she could find the privacy she needed to pull herself back into a semblance of a human being.

She slipped off her coat and kicked her wet shoes under the chair. She looked like a drowned rat. A heavy rain had started as she left the motel office, soaking her hair and skin. She was thankful her coat had kept her clothes dry.

The desk clerk hadn't asked questions. He had registered her and handed her the key that made running too simple. She could still see Eli's face when she told him the truth and rushed away.

She closed her eyes as the memories poured in. New memories, happy ones of Eli, Lynnie, her day care center, Granny. No doubt her friend would be worried sick.

Diedra paced the room, turning on the television to drive out the loneliness. It had been awhile since pain had engulfed her to this degree. Ever since Eli had come into her life, Diedra realized, clenching her hands until her nails made crescent-shaped cuts in her palms.

How could she have done this to him? She felt like such a bad person. She covered her ears as the accusations taunted her.

"No!" Her scream echoed in the room. She didn't want to

hurt Eli. *But you hurt him,* the voice whispered. *You hurt him. You hurt him. . . .*

Unable to bear the agony, Diedra crumpled on the floor. The pressure gripped her head like a vise. She cried for her baby, for Eli, Lynnie, her family, herself, and all she'd lost, sobbing until she could barely lift her head.

Minutes turned into hours until slowly the trancelike state receded. A glance at her watch confirmed the late hour. She had to call Granny. She went to the bathroom and splashed cold water on her face. She stared at her mussed hair. Uncaring, she turned from the mirror. Moving like a sleepwalker, she returned to the bedroom.

When Granny picked up the phone, Diedra said, "It's me."

"Dee. Where are you?"

"I'm okay."

"Eli's looking for you."

Pain hit like an unexpected stomach punch. "I know. He asked me to marry him, to provide a family for Lynnie. I've never hated Benjamin more than I do at this moment."

"You don't mean that, Dee," Granny said softly. "Where are you? You shouldn't be alone."

"Don't ask. Please."

"God will bring you through this, Dee. Trust in Him."

She allowed the tears to fall freely. "How can God love me when I have so much hate in my heart?"

"He loves us, faults and all. And He'll help you find forgiveness if you ask. Eli's here now," Granny said. "At least speak to him."

She swallowed hard. "Put him on."

As she listened to the phone exchange hands, she accepted that Eli had broken through her fragile barrier. No matter how hard she tried, she would never forget him.

"Diedra, sweetheart, where are you?"

Painful emotion lodged in her throat. "I have to think."

He sighed heavily, his voice so filled with anguish she could barely understand his words. "I love you."

"I love you, too, but I should have told you."

"We can work this out," he insisted.

Oh, how she wished that were true. "Eli, please know this has nothing to do with you," Diedra said. "You're one of the few truly loving people I've known in my life. You deserve the best."

With that she cut him off, removing the last trace of happiness from her world.

❧

Eli held Lynnie close as he removed the bottle from her mouth. "Where is she?" he asked. Just hearing her pain had pierced like a knife through his heart.

"I'd say in town," Granny said. "She's probably found a place where she can grieve."

"This situation is not insurmountable," Eli insisted.

"To her it is."

He held Lynnie against his chest as he stood. "I need to find her. I know what she's feeling. She's hurting just as Kelly did."

"Maybe," Granny said. "But we need to give her time."

"That's the one thing I have plenty of," Eli said. "There will never be anyone else for me."

"God will work this out for you."

"I believe that, Granny. As you told Dee, He loves us faults and all. He put her in my life for a reason. I know that much. I love her."

"And she loves you. Let's pray for her."

Eli reached out and clasped Granny's hand in his. Together

they bowed in prayer. Granny squeezed his hand. "Diedra will come home soon."

⁂

Diedra awoke disoriented and frightened, staring at the strange room, aware of someone knocking at the door.

"Please, no," she breathed as everything rushed in on her. Eli couldn't have found her already. She needed more time.

Diedra crawled from the bed, frowning at her disheveled state. She staggered to the door and looked through the peephole, relieved to find the motel cleaning staff. She told the woman she didn't need her services. Closing the door, Diedra wondered what she was going to do. After Benjamin, determination had kept her going. What would give her that needed push now?

Anger toward Benjamin and her parents had pushed her into the new life she'd found with her grandparents. Her parents had never uttered one word of argument, never attempted to heal the rift between them.

She'd loved them, and they hurt her. She couldn't do the same to Eli. Already she'd done so much damage. Selfishly she'd allowed the love to grow, all the while knowing she should walk away. Diedra couldn't deny Eli a family. She couldn't see him again. Making him hate her was her only option. She was afraid. Afraid she wouldn't be strong enough to say no. Too afraid he could convince her it didn't matter. Maybe it didn't now, but one day it could.

Eli and Kelly had gone to extremes for Lynnie, and Diedra couldn't believe that having more children wouldn't matter to him. She sat in the room's only chair.

Diedra leaned her head back and dropped her arm across her eyes as the pain knotted in her stomach. She had to do this. No matter how much she hurt. No matter how long it took her to get over her loss. No matter if she never got over him. She had no other choice.

❧

Eli rubbed his eyes, feeling the results of his sleepless night. Agonizing hours, filled with thoughts of Diedra and the total devastation on her face when she'd told him she was barren. In a way he wanted to be angry because Diedra hadn't trusted him enough to tell him earlier, and yet Eli understood because of Kelly. If only he had pushed a little harder for her to talk.

He recalled her response to his question about babies. She had alluded to the possibility. How it must have hurt to know that even if she wanted them, she could never have children of her own.

He loved Diedra far too much to lose her, and he'd fight as much as he needed to in order to get her back. He could convince her. As soon as he found her.

He dropped Lynnie off at the center and went to his office early. After a few minutes Eli knew he couldn't wait out the hours there either. He had to do something. He ripped a listing of hotels and motels from the phone book and took off. Two hours and he didn't know how many hotels and motels later, he dialed the office again.

"Janice, have you heard anything yet?"

"No, and I'm not likely to if you keep calling every few minutes," she told him.

"I have to find her." He grew more desperate by the minute. "Pray she doesn't hurt herself."

"Keep searching, Eli. I'll call the minute I know anything."

He tossed his phone onto the seat next to him and glanced at the dashboard to find the gas needle dancing over the empty mark. Pulling into a gas station, he propped against the car and squeezed the nozzle handle hard, as if doing so would make the gas flow faster. The next motel on the list was in this neighborhood.

He straightened and looked around. The area could do with renovation. He saw old restaurants with rusting signs, businesses that had changed hands so often the new owners had tacked signs over the larger painted names rather than bothering to paint. People wandered the streets as if they had nowhere to be. He hoped Diedra hadn't come here. It didn't look safe.

The aged motel sign caught Eli's eye. He glanced toward the parking lot, skipping over the cars that weren't the exact shade of blue as hers.

A transfer truck drove past, blocking Eli's view. He looked at the numbers on the pump. How long would this take? He sighed.

The vehicle passed, and Eli resumed his search, starting on the opposite side of the lot. His gaze drifted along then darted back, stopping on the far corner. It had to be hers. The color was right, and the rear door panel was dented in the same spot where a parent had backed into her car a couple of weeks before.

Eli shoved the gas nozzle into the holder. He ran inside and tossed a twenty onto the counter. "Keep the change."

Cutting across the street in the traffic, Eli was oblivious to the blaring horns and loud insults. He parked in front of the office and ran inside.

Despite all his pleading and badgering, the desk clerk stood firm in his refusal to give Eli the room number and threatened to call the police if he didn't leave.

Frustrated, Eli stepped outside. One of these doors hid Diedra from him. He fought the temptation to knock on every one of them until he found her. "Please, God," he prayed, "help me find her. Show me the way."

Eli could hardly believe his eyes when Diedra exited a room, carrying an ice bucket. He whispered his thanks before running toward her. "Dee," he called gently.

She stopped and looked at him. "Hello, Eli."

He felt overwhelming relief as his gaze swept over her, ignoring the stringy, uncombed hair, slept-in clothing, and red puffiness around her eyes. He wanted to touch her, to assure himself she was real. But Eli knew she wouldn't let him. "I love you. Please come home."

Diedra dropped her head. "I can't."

"Why not?" he asked sharply. He'd vowed to be patient, and yet he was already snapping at her. "I'm sorry. Forgive me."

Diedra tucked loose strands of hair behind her ears. "Don't, Eli. If anyone should apologize, it's me."

"Tell me why, Dee. I have to know."

She indicated two chairs by the pool. She sat down, placing the ice bucket on the nearby table.

"Have you eaten? Would you like to go somewhere for coffee?"

She shook her head. Eli sat opposite her.

"Why, Dee?"

"I can't be the mother of your children, Eli. I won't deprive you of the opportunity to be the wonderful father I know you are."

"I don't care if we can't have children. It doesn't matter."

"It does!" Diedra cried out, total despair hiding the loveliness of her face. "It matters a great deal to me."

"Dee, I understand," Eli whispered. "Kelly felt the same way. She wanted to divorce me so I could find a woman to give me children. I didn't want another woman. And I don't want another one now. I want you. Another woman can't fill your place in my heart."

Diedra looked up at him. "I lost a piece of myself when my unborn child was murdered. I'll never know what it is to hold my child in my arms."

Eli wanted to cry for her. All the time she'd loved his child, she'd been grieving for her own unborn child. "What happened, Dee?"

A pained look crossed her face. "My husband took offense at the news of my pregnancy. He slapped me so hard I fell backward down a flight of stairs. The banister broke, and the bottom rail impaled me."

The scars he had seen. And more he hadn't. Her husband had put them there. "Oh, honey, I'm so sorry," Eli murmured, reaching out to her.

She looked down, ignoring his hands. "Don't pity me, Eli. It wasn't the first time Benjamin abused me. It started on our wedding night. I was a textbook case. I kept making excuses for him. He was tired. I'd done something to upset him. He didn't mean to hurt me. Then I accepted the truth and went to my father. He sent me back to Benjamin. He said the lies would destroy my husband's career. My father called me a liar.

"The night it happened, I lay on the floor thinking I would die while Benjamin ranted and raved that the accident was my fault. It took him a long time to dial 911. The hospital staff called the police. I filed charges the day they told me my baby was dead.

"When my parents found out, they pressed me to drop the case. They said everything would be easier if it didn't appear in the press." She looked at him. "Easier for whom? Certainly not me."

"Dee, I've experienced the side of your nature that doesn't give up on people. Loving like that makes you vulnerable."

"I've dealt with the self-pity, Eli. Now my strength comes from God and the work He gives me to do. I can't let anything destroy that, or I'll be destroyed, too."

"I understand."

"I think you do," she agreed.

"Just remember you don't have to give birth to a child to love it."

For an instant, wistfulness stole into her expression.

"If having a child of your own doesn't really matter, why did you give in to Kelly?"

Eli hesitated. "I—I don't—"

"Why, Eli?" she persisted.

He owed her the truth. "Because Kelly insisted I be the father," he admitted. "She wouldn't accept anything less. I didn't want to lose her."

The sadness in Diedra's eyes tore at his heart. "I want children, too, but I can have only those who belong to other people. I'm angry, Eli, and until I deal with that anger, I can't love anyone as they need to be loved."

"You can. You already have," he said softly. "You've made a difference for me." He reached out to her. "Let me help you."

Diedra shook her head. "My emotions have controlled the situation for too long. I took something I had no right to take."

"You took what I freely gave," Eli said. "And you gave so much more than you took."

"It's not that simple, Eli."

Eli didn't want to frighten her with his desperation. "You think I didn't know something wasn't right? I should have pushed, but I never figured we couldn't handle whatever it was when the situation arose. You're an intelligent woman. You know it won't be simple, but we can work together."

Diedra pulled her overcoat tighter about her.

"Are you sure you don't want to get something to eat?"

She shook her head. "You'd think I was intelligent. High school valedictorian, summa cum laude college graduate, and a master's degree in education. But I refused to admit failure, and it cost me dearly.

"I tried to be a good wife. Benjamin was demanding, ruthless, overbearing. Nothing I did pleased him. I took it over and over until the night I nearly died. I kept trying to prove I could make it better, while Benjamin beat every ounce of love from me."

Anger shone in Eli's eyes. "Diedra, you don't have to—"

"I do, Eli. You have to know the demon I'm fighting. I accepted my failure as a wife and got on with the successful parts; but no matter how hard I try, my other successes can't compensate. I'm an angry failure, and I won't let myself hurt you, Eli."

She stood and started to walk away.

He jumped up and stepped in front of her. "You can't blame yourself, Diedra," he said, reaching out and grasping her hand. Tears filled his eyes. He drew a deep breath then pulled her to him. "You married a batterer. He wasn't capable of making his own life work, much less yours. With God's help and our love for one another, we can work this out. Are you sure there's no chance you can conceive?"

"Benjamin did the job well," she whispered. "The doctors used lots of technical terms, but the end result's the same."

"Have you ever seen Benjamin again or told him how angry you are?"

"I can't, Eli."

"You have to. You can't bottle these emotions inside. You're still afraid of the power he held over you."

Diedra rested her head against his shoulder. "Benjamin

died following a long, difficult battle with cancer. He sent for me, but I refused to go."

"Oh." Eli was silent a moment. "What about counseling?" he finally asked.

She shook her head. "I went. I thought I'd worked everything out in my head. Then I met you, and things fell apart again."

"Oh, Dee, what will it take to convince you? You love me—us—and we love you. Let that be a beginning."

"Until I deal with this, there's a part of me I can't give. I have so much hate in my heart. I have to forgive, but I can't."

"God knows your heart, Dee. He knows you want to forgive and move on. Sweetheart, you showed me love. Let me do the same for you."

"I can't deny you more children, Eli. I just can't."

"We have Lynnie. She's enough."

Diedra shook her head and pulled away. She buried her face in her hands. "I can't. Not now."

"At least come home," Eli said. Diedra needed the routine of her life to fight this battle. And if it meant giving her up until she was ready, he would. "I promise not to push you to make a decision."

A police car pulled into the parking lot, and an officer got out and walked into the office. A minute later he came toward them.

"Is everything okay, miss?" he asked Diedra, glancing at Eli. She nodded.

"It's all right, Officer. I'm leaving," Eli told him. "Please come home, Dee."

"I'll think about it."

"Do that, please, and think about us. Life does go on, and you deserve to be happy."

fifteen

"Dee?" Granny's voice floated up the stairs. "Eli's here. May he come up?"

Diedra closed her eyes and sighed. Granny had asked the same question every day this week, and Diedra had responded in the same way. "Lynnie's in the crib. I'll be in my room."

"I'm not coming up," Eli called. "Are you okay?"

The question stabbed at her heart. She might never be okay again. She loved Eli and wanted to run down those stairs and let him make her world perfect. *But who would make his world perfect for him?* Diedra asked herself as Gina lifted Lynnie from the crib and started down the stairs. Certainly not her.

Diedra knew Eli struggled to understand, to be patient. But she doubted he'd wait forever. Fearful images built in her mind. If the past few days were an example of what life without Eli would be like, she knew she couldn't survive the future.

You deserve to be happy.

The words were as clear as the night Eli had spoken them. No amount of thinking, of trying to justify the part she'd played in putting herself in this situation, could change the truth, and Diedra accepted that. Life had no certainties and no promises, and no matter how much she loved Eli, she couldn't risk having him hate her because she'd denied him the love he deserved.

Diedra clutched her stomach in a useless attempt to stifle the emptiness. Her world had come to a standstill. Not even Kids Unlimited could fill the void, and that scared her. Not one day went by that she didn't miss Eli McKay even more than the day before.

❧

"How is she, Granny?" Eli asked as he turned from the stairs. It hurt that she wouldn't talk to him, but he refused to give up hope.

"I don't know," she said, shaking her graying head. "Diedra's withdrawing more daily. This place used to be her life, but she rarely comes downstairs. She's not taking care of herself. I'm worried."

Eli grimaced and massaged his forehead. He hated feeling useless. "I want to help, but short of storming upstairs and shaking some sense into her, I don't know what to do." He swallowed the lump that rose in his throat.

"You're helping. More than you know. This thing has simmered in the background for years. Like dynamite waiting to explode."

"And I provided the fire," Eli said with a grim look.

"Fire tempered with love," Granny said. "Diedra loves you, but she's more afraid of what she can't give you than what she can."

He looked at her. "She can love me. That's all I want."

"I'm glad to hear you say that. Diedra needs the love of a special man. One who is capable of returning her love. One who can accept that her past is a part of their future."

Eli lifted Lynnie from Gina's arms, smiling absently at the woman before he greeted his daughter. Lynnie smiled at him.

I envy you, sweetie, he thought. *You get to be in Diedra's arms, and I want so badly to be there, too.*

After Gina left, Eli said, "I'm trying to understand, Granny. I really am."

"Diedra thought she'd managed to put it all behind her."

The baby's smiles and arm-waving brought a smile to his own face. "When I brought Lynnie here, I wondered if this was best for her. I had no idea it would be best for us both. I pray for Dee several times a day."

A smile curved Granny's lips. "Diedra will come out of it. You'll see. We've let this go too long. Let me tell you what I have in mind."

ॐ

Diedra dried the tears of the latest grief session and went into the bathroom to splash cold water on her face.

"Diedra? Where are you?"

"In the bathroom."

"I'll wait for you in the sitting room. We need to discuss something," Granny said.

Diedra sucked in a deep breath and stared at the pitiful reflection in the mirror. "Granny, you know—"

"I'm not talking through a closed door," the older woman said. "There's been enough hiding around here."

Diedra threw the door open. "I'm not hiding!"

Granny sighed. "You've been hiding from the world for a week now. Or perhaps I should say from Eli McKay."

Diedra nodded her head and followed Granny into the sitting room. She settled on the couch, pulled up her legs, and wrapped her arms around them. "It hurts, Granny. It hurts so much."

"Ignoring the circumstances won't change anything. You can't even put the situation in the proper perspective until you admit that. Your inability to have children is a fact. Eli loves you, Diedra. He loves you a lot, and you're breaking his heart."

"He asked me to marry him, Granny. To help him give Lynnie the family she needs."

"Did you ask what he meant by that?"

"He wants a wife and children."

"Family has more than one definition. A man, a wife, and a child can be a family. What makes you think you couldn't be enough for him? He told me his wife had suffered as you are now."

Diedra's head filled with the things Eli had said to her after learning she couldn't have children. Could he really want her as a wife, a mother to his daughter?

"I know you haven't asked for my advice, but I have some for you anyway," Granny said. "First off, start praying and quit moping. If you're determined to deprive yourself of Eli's love and that's what God directs you to do, tell Eli and be done with him. Then get yourself straightened out. You can't solve the abuse matter alone. Go see a counselor.

"But if you want any kind of future, you'll welcome Eli McKay and his daughter into your heart. Put the past where it belongs. We have few second chances in life. There's no changing the past, but you can change your future with God's help."

Diedra hesitated. "I feel as though I'm cheating him. From the first I knew I shouldn't get involved, but my feelings for him prodded me on. For every step back I took, the emotions knocked me forward two. I didn't ask for God's guidance. I knew it wouldn't work; yet I couldn't refuse myself just one more minute with Eli. I took from Eli until it was too late, and now I'm hurting him."

"You're cheating him of your love."

The truth hurt. Unable to sit still any longer, Diedra jumped up to pace the room. "I hate myself for letting it happen, Granny. I never wanted to hurt Eli. I want to love him."

"Then show him."

"You really think it doesn't matter?" Doubt pervaded her voice.

"I think you could heal each other."

Diedra stopped in front of Granny. "I owe everyone an apology."

"We love you, Dee. The others don't know the full story, but they've stood by you every step of the way. Gina's even planning to postpone her move for a few months."

The idea of interfering with the happiness of yet another person horrified Diedra. "No. She shouldn't waste one minute of the time she can spend with the man she loves. Is she still here?"

Granny nodded. "Downstairs."

"I'm going to talk to her."

"That's my girl," Granny said. "Get on with life. Your world has been missing you. Can we pray first?"

Diedra nodded, bowing her head as they sought solace from their heavenly Father.

"Dear Lord," Granny began, her voice calling out to the One who could make things right. "We come to You tonight praising and thanking You for the love You freely give. We ask that You touch Diedra's life and heal her. Empower her to be able to forgive and grow in Your love each day. Help her to build a life with Eli that is both happy and pleasing to You. Amen."

Diedra spent the next hour convincing Gina she wouldn't allow her to change her plans. Afterward she went into the office and picked up the job applications. Granny made a lot of sense. Her grief served no purpose. She had a life to live, kids to care for, decisions to make.

Diedra made herself comfortable on the couch and began reviewing the applicants. Thoughts of Eli resting in this very spot the first time they met filled her head. Dropping the papers in her lap, she pleaded, "Lord, please tell me what to do."

She felt an overwhelming urge to share her fears and doubts with Eli. As she drove to his house, Diedra wondered how Eli would react to what she had to tell him. She wanted to give him all the love she had to give but knew overcoming the past would take no less than the miracle of God's love.

At the house, the length of the sidewalk seemed to double and then triple as she covered the few steps to the porch. Diedra hesitated. "You're a coward," she chided herself then pressed the doorbell.

She heard footsteps treading across the marble floor then saw light flooding the window. The deadbolt clicked, and the door opened slowly.

Diedra's heart lurched as she stared at Eli. His blue eyes had lost some of their sparkle, and shadows lay beneath them. "May I come in?"

Eli held the door wide. "Is everything okay?"

"It's going to be," Diedra said.

Eli smiled and opened his arms to her. "Thank You, Lord!"

She loved this man. Even after all the hurt she'd inflicted, he still cared. "I'm sorry."

The house came to life with the sounds of Lynnie's stirring on the sound system. "You want me to get her?" Diedra asked.

He gathered her close, shaking his head. "Do you have any idea how much I've missed you?" he asked, his arms tightening as if he were afraid she'd disappear.

"Probably as much as I've missed you," Diedra admitted, wiggling to loosen his hold. "A bit of me has died every day since I sent you away, but I wanted to be fair."

"When will you be fair to yourself, Dee? You're not responsible for all the wrongs in your world."

She touched his cheek. Eli pulled her hand to his mouth and kissed it.

"I realized I'm still grieving, too. I thought I was past the hurt. Everything was fine as long as I focused on work, you, and Lynnie, anything but myself. My child would have been five years old," she said. "I'll never be able to give you a child, and that hurts more than anything else. I don't think I could bear it if you ever came to hate me."

"Hate you? Dee, darling, do you know what just thinking about not having you in my life did to me?" Eli said. "You shut me out."

"I need you to love me, Eli," Diedra replied in a tiny, frightened voice. "But I need to know the truth about how you feel about never having more children. I'll leave right now if there's the slightest possibility you could be unhappy because we can't."

His mood seemed suddenly buoyant. "But, darling, we have a child. And she needs two parents."

"Is that what you meant by making a family for Lynnie?"

"I meant whatever we could have," Eli said. "I didn't know the truth, but it doesn't change the way I feel about you. I'd want you even if I didn't have Lynnie. Even if it meant never becoming a father. I love you, Dee."

Tears of joy slipped down Diedra's face. "Then if you don't mind, I'd like to give my love to you and your daughter for the remaining time we have."

Diedra entwined her fingers with his. "I plan to see a counselor. There will be times when I'm unrealistic, unreasonable, and withdrawn. Times when the past will bear down on me in ways I can't handle."

"And I'll be right by your side, loving and supporting you in every way I can. Understand I'm here to help lessen the burden. Talk to me. Trust me to share the bad things in your life. Know I'll stand by you no matter what."

"I do trust you," she whispered, her fingers tightening around his. "I should have told you the truth."

"You couldn't. I know you wanted to. Your child's death was not your fault. Don't you see, Dee? Life does go on. I'm offering you a package deal. What's wrong with being my wife and providing Lynnie with a mother's love?"

"I can't think of a thing," Diedra whispered. "I already love Lynnie as my own. She's the most special child at Kids Unlimited."

"Spoken like a true new mother." He hugged her close.

"You're giving me motherhood, Eli," she said with a soft smile, "though maybe not in the conventional manner."

"I need you in my life. With God's help it's going to work for us."

"It will," Diedra agreed. "Everything that makes you happy is all I want. Can you understand that's what this has been about?"

"You make me happy, Diedra."

"Then I love you, and I'll marry you."

"I've wanted to hear that," Eli said, kissing her gently.

Diedra became aware of the baby's noises over the sound system. She tilted her head slightly, listening to Lynnie. "Eli, she's laughing."

His face was transformed, and his voice sent shivers over her. "See—I told you. Our happiness extends all over this house."

Her arms went around his neck. "I love you, Eli."

"Welcome home, Dee," he whispered.

sixteen

The next morning Eli arrived at the center to find Diedra in the nursery, already hard at work supervising the volunteer grandparents who were feeding and cuddling the babies. He ignored the interested stares of the others in the room when he kissed her. "Good morning, sweetheart."

Diedra nodded and smiled.

"So when are we going to make our engagement official?" Eli asked.

"The day I mark the last item off my list."

"What list?" Eli asked, puzzled by her comment. She hadn't mentioned a list the previous evening when they talked.

"Overachievers make lists. It helps keep us focused on the tasks at hand."

He could handle that. "So what can I do to help you get this list completed as quickly as possible?"

Diedra glanced over her shoulder at Granny, who had just entered the room. "Granny, could you take care of things here for a few minutes?"

Granny smiled. "Good morning, Eli. I'm glad to see you both looking so happy."

Eli's hand wrapped around Diedra's waist. "Not as happy are we are to feel that way."

Diedra led him to the office. "I've made a list of the things I feel I need to do before I can make it official. I crossed off the first item this morning when I called the domestic violence shelter. I spoke with the director and requested a counselor referral. We talked for some time, and she suggested I attend their group sessions. She says I've taken the first step. I believe her."

"I'm glad," Eli said, hugging her. "I know how difficult that must have been for you."

Diedra nodded. "I also bought a plane ticket. I'm going to visit my parents."

Eli spoke without hesitation. "I'm going with you."

"What about Lynnie and your business?"

Eli knew she was trying to give him an out. "I'll ask Granny and Janice to help out. It's important that I be with you."

Later that afternoon on the plane, Diedra felt her love for Eli deepening. Once they arrived at the airport, she called her mother, and Eli rented a car and drove them to her parents' home.

"Are you okay?" Eli asked, his hand covering hers after they parked in the circular drive.

Diedra felt no great emotion at returning home for the first time in five years.

"Impressive," Eli said, looking around at the property.

Everything appeared perfect, from the roof of the three-story mansion to the beautifully landscaped lawn. Her parents had never planned one detail or planted one flower. The staff did everything. Her parents couldn't be bothered.

"I always thought it was ugly. This place never seemed like a home in the truest sense of the word." She smiled faintly. "Ready to meet your future in-laws?"

"You bet." He jumped out of the car and went around to open her door. Eli held on to her as they walked up the front steps and stopped before the heavy wooden door. "Ready?"

She nodded, and he reached to ring the doorbell. The butler greeted them, and Eli held on to Diedra's hand. It hurt her that there was no joyous reception upon her arrival. The man showed them into the drawing room where Diedra's mother waited.

"Diedra, do come in," her mother said when they paused in the doorway. Her gaze touched on their connected hands. "Are you going to introduce your friend?"

"This is my fiancé, Eli McKay."

Her mother's expression showed nothing. "Please have a seat. Your father's taking an important call. He'll be with us shortly."

His daughter has come home for the first time in years. Would it have been too much to ask someone to take a message? Diedra thought critically. Silence loomed as they all sat uncomfortably, waiting and wondering who would voice the next words.

"How long have you and—?" her mother began.

"Eli," Diedra supplied, angry that her mother pretended not to remember his name. "Elijah McKay."

"How long have you been engaged?" she asked, glancing at Diedra's left hand.

"Not long."

"Have you set a date for the wedding?"

"No. We have issues to work through first."

"There's no need to rush into anything."

The censure in her words didn't go unnoticed. As they continued their roles of polite strangers, Diedra couldn't help but wonder if her mother had ever cared about anything but propriety. Still, she refused to offer the words that would make Eli socially acceptable.

No doubt her mother would put aside her disdain if she knew Eli was a successful executive.

Tired of the verbal fencing, Diedra said bluntly, "We hope to marry soon."

The door opened, and her father stepped into the room. Diedra noted her mother's relief when she stood quickly and approached him. "James, this is Diedra's fiancé, Eli McKay."

"Diedra, Mr. McKay," her father said in curt acknowledgment of their presence as he joined his wife on the sofa opposite them.

"Mr. Wynne," Eli said with a nod.

"Hello, Daddy," Diedra said, her voice tight with emotion. "I suppose you and Mother wonder why I arranged this visit."

Her father frowned. "This is your home, Diedra."

"I haven't considered it my home for a long time."

"If you're trying to make a point, perhaps we should go into the study." His words were cold, overly polite. "And discuss the matter privately."

"No." Diedra shook her head and reached for Eli's hand. "I want Eli to hear this. My past affects him as much as it does me. I have to get rid of the anger I feel so we can get on with our lives."

"Diedra, it's past. Forget it," her mother said.

Terrible bitterness assailed Diedra. "How, Mother? How do I forget your accusations that I turned Granny and Gramps against you because of what Benjamin did to me? Did you really think I'd do something like that to spite you?"

"I won't have you speaking to your mother that way, Diedra."

Aghast, she turned to her father. "And you, Daddy, how will I forgive you for calling me a liar and sending me back to Benjamin?"

Her father's discomfort was obvious. He glanced at his wife and back at Diedra. "I had no idea of Benjamin's instabilities."

"Why didn't you believe me? Did you really think I would fabricate such a story? That I was some pampered little brat who came crying to Daddy because my husband spoke harshly to me?"

"You were happy at first," he said. "I couldn't help but feel some of the glitter had worn off."

Diedra stood up. "Oh, it wore off. Benjamin revealed his true colors on our wedding night. It's a good thing we were gone for two weeks. It took that long for the bruises to fade. But that's not why I'm here. Benjamin Pierce is dead. My marriage cost me a great deal, but you know that as well as I. Perhaps you even grieved a little for your grandchild."

"Diedra, I didn't know why his mother wanted money," her father replied in a low, tormented voice. "We were on a business trip when she called the office and said Benjamin needed money. I had my accountant write the check. We didn't know. You hadn't contacted us."

"I was fighting for my life in the hospital," Diedra said.

Strain marks appeared around her parents' tight lips. "Do you think we ever forget that?" her father asked.

"But you wanted me to drop the charges."

Her father's face was bleak with sorrow. "The press was having a field day. You were struggling physically and mentally. I felt it would be easier for you to handle the matter privately. A quiet divorce, and Benjamin would disappear from your life."

"And reappear in the life of another unsuspecting woman? I couldn't let that happen. I did what I had to do. The court forced Benjamin to seek help. Women need to speak up."

"I know that now, Diedra," her father said. "We wanted to protect you. Saying we're sorry probably doesn't mean much at this point, but we are."

"I don't want you to be sorry," Diedra said. "I want you to love me for who I am. With Granny and Gramps I didn't have to excel. I could be me, and for a long time I was no prize. Loving Eli has taught me I don't have to work so hard at pleasing everyone." Tears filled her eyes as she glanced at him then looked at her parents again. "I love you both, but I've spent years believing you didn't care. And you let me."

"We thought it best to stay out of your life."

"Because it was better not to have your errant daughter where people could pity her?"

"We don't deserve your anger, Diedra," her father said. "Maybe your mother and I aren't parents of the year, but you've never wanted for anything."

"Just one thing," she whispered. "I wanted your love. I felt guilty for not being the daughter you wanted. The trial and then Mother's reaction to the will magnified the feeling. I have to get past this to move on with my life. I wanted you to meet Eli. We're here to invite you to be part of our family— parents and in-laws."

"And grandparents," Eli added.

Her parents' eyes widened.

"If you'd like to visit, we'd love to introduce you to our daughter," Eli said.

Our daughter. Those were beautiful words to Diedra's ears. Eli had brought up the subject of adoption during the flight. As soon as they married, he planned to start the proceedings to see that Diedra McKay officially became Gerilyn Marie McKay's mother.

"Do you have a picture?" Diedra's mother asked softly.

Eli pulled out his wallet and handed her a photo of Diedra and Lynnie. "She's ten months old," he volunteered. "Her name is Lynnie."

Diedra's father studied the picture closely and handed it back to Eli. "Diedra will make an excellent mother."

"Yes, sir," Eli agreed, grasping Diedra's hand. "She's very good with children. Her day care center has an excellent reputation."

"You turned the house into a day care center?" her mother asked, looking shocked.

"That's what Granny and Gramps wanted. They helped me get started."

"Kids Unlimited," Eli said proudly. "You've never seen a place more filled with love."

"Diedra, I'm so sorry," her mother whispered as she stood and opened her arms. "Can you forgive us?"

Tears poured down Diedra's face as she allowed her mother to hug her close. "Yes."

"May we come to the wedding?" She glanced at her husband. "We'd like to be there."

Diedra sniffed and laughed as she accepted the handkerchief her father passed her. "We're not sending out invitations. The guests will be our loved ones and friends. I'll let you know when we set the date."

Her mother insisted they stay for dinner. They refused the offer of overnight accommodations to catch their eleven o'clock flight. Diedra knew it would take a long time for them to get beyond the pain, but at least they were on speaking terms again.

Later they sat in the car, Diedra wrapped in Eli's arms as she shed a few tears of joy. His embrace provided the comfort and security she'd needed so desperately. She didn't know how she had survived so long without him.

"I was a little nervous during those first few minutes," Eli said. "Your parents on one sofa and us on the other. I thought we were choosing up sides."

Diedra laughed at his apt description. "What do you think of your future in-laws?"

"With a daughter like you, they can't be all bad." Eli cupped Diedra's chin in his hand. "It's going to be okay."

She hugged him tighter. "I believe that, too."

They returned the rental car and went to the airport coffee shop to wait for their flight. On board they found their assigned seats. Diedra waited while Eli secured his belt and made himself comfortable in the seat.

She leaned her head against his shoulder. "I have a favor to ask. I want you to take me to a race."

He looked at her. "I didn't know you liked racing."

Diedra rested her hand on his arm. "I don't know if I do either. But you do, and I want to see what you like."

Eli shrugged. "Sure, if that's what you want."

"It is," she said with a degree of satisfaction. "By the way, I'm going to make an appointment with my doctor."

He sat up straighter. "Dee? You don't need to do this."

She touched his cheek. "I do."

❧

A month later Diedra prepared dinner in Eli's kitchen while Lynnie banged on pots with a wooden spatula nearby.

Eli entered the room and stepped over to her. "What did the doctor say?"

Diedra stopped chopping tomatoes and smiled at him. She shook her head, feeling the familiar knot lodge in her throat. "She said what we already knew."

Eli's eyes clouded with tears. Diedra knew he wanted the news to be different for her sake. His arms wrapped around her waist, and he pulled her to rest against him. "Are you okay?"

Diedra relished the security she felt. "God has been very good to me. You and Lynnie are all I need."

"You're all I need."

"And how did you do?" Diedra asked, speaking of his errand for the day.

"Sweetheart, giving money away is never a problem. McKay Showrooms is now a proud sponsor."

Diedra hugged him, enjoying the glow of excitement on his face. Eli had finally admitted he loved racing. They had attended a couple of races as fans then gone to see his friend race.

She was glad when his buddy convinced Eli to give his new car a spin around the track. On the way home he had acknowledged he'd enjoyed himself. "But my competitive edge is gone. I didn't think about winning. I thought about how much life I missed while I focused on racing. I don't want to go back to that."

"I don't care what you do as long as you realize you have an obligation to yourself, to your own happiness. Everything else, Lynnie, me, the business, should add to that feeling, not weigh you down."

"I know. I recognized your ploy from the beginning."

"And I thought I was being sneaky."

He laughed. "You were about as obvious as a speeding bus. I did push racing into the background, all the time pretending it didn't make any difference. Lately it seems I enjoy the business more, though. Probably because I'm happy in my personal life."

Excitement filled her with the words. Diedra knew exactly what he meant. Eli encouraged her participation in the spousal abuse group meetings, urging her to share her experiences with the other women who thought they could make things better. Counseling convinced Diedra that the abuse wasn't her fault and that her self-blame served no purpose.

They'd even gone to couples' counseling. Knowing Eli loved her enough to be there for her when she needed him had helped Diedra see she was worth loving.

"We need to finish here," Diedra said. "Janice is bringing Kaylie and Davey over."

"I'm going to fire that woman," Eli said with a frown.

She laughed at his frown. "Janice promised to keep Lynnie while we're on our honeymoon."

"In that case I'll have to give her a bonus."

Diedra laughed. "Oh, you're crazy about Davey. And you don't mind having him over."

"The kid's a character. He's getting worse by the day."

"And you're doing your share to help. What were you and David thinking last week when you sent him into the kitchen to get those chips? Janice said she's still finding them everywhere."

"David sent him," Eli said. "How were we supposed to know he'd try to open the bag the way his dad does?"

"He had to climb up on the counter."

"Janice yelled at him," Eli added with a grin.

"And then she yelled at you and David," Diedra said, bursting into laughter. "Are you sure it's wise to let him be Lynnie's friend?"

"Our daughter knows a champ when she sees one," Eli said. "You see the way she follows him around?"

"Soaking it up like a sponge," Diedra supplied. "Have you forgiven me for her first word being *Mama*?"

Eli threw back his head and roared with laughter. "Why do you persist in believing that gibberish is *Mama*?"

"We're working on *Daddy* now," she said, draping her arms around his neck.

"I love you," he said.

Diedra's eyes brightened with pleasure. He could never say those words too many times for her. "I love you, Eli. More than I can ever express."

"I can't wait to put my ring on your finger and call you my wife."

"Our wedding day will be here before you know it."

epilogue

The groom wore a black tuxedo and waited at the base of the staircase. His best girl was dressed in pink organza and sat in Janice's lap. The ring bearer played with the pillow, holding it upside down and swinging the ribbon-tied rings back and forth.

Their audience was alive with the assorted fidgeting of Diedra's honorary attendants in their child-sized chairs. It was standing room only as parents, staff, and other guests filled every available space on the ground floor of the day care center's hallway. Diedra's mother sat in the front row, looking spectacular in an ice-blue designer gown.

The music began, and Eli lifted his eyes to where the love of his life would soon make her entrance. Granny Marie moved slowly down the stairs that were garlanded with greenery, pink roses, white ribbon, and twinkling fairy lights.

The music changed, and Diedra appeared at the top of the stairs holding her father's arm. Eli admired the elegant gown and noted she carried the bouquet of miniature white roses he'd sent up to her earlier. Diedra wore her mother's veil, made of exquisite lace that couldn't mask what he considered an even more exquisite face.

His gaze never wavered, and when she came to a stop by his side, Diedra smiled up at him. "Dearly beloved" was all Eli heard as he grasped her hand in his and returned the smile. They had come full circle. With God's help they had looked to the heart and found what they both once believed could never be.

A Letter To Our Readers

Dear Reader:

In order that we might better contribute to your reading enjoyment, we would appreciate your taking a few minutes to respond to the following questions. We welcome your comments and read each form and letter we receive. When completed, please return to the following:

Fiction Editor
Heartsong Presents
PO Box 719
Uhrichsville, Ohio 44683

1. Did you enjoy reading *Look to the Heart* by Terry Fowler?
   ❏ Very much! I would like to see more books by this author!
   ❏ Moderately. I would have enjoyed it more if

   _____

   _____

   _____

2. Are you a member of **Heartsong Presents**? ❏ Yes ❏ No
   If no, where did you purchase this book? _____

   _____

3. How would you rate, on a scale from 1 (poor) to 5 (superior), the cover design? _____

4. On a scale from 1 (poor) to 10 (superior), please rate the following elements.

   ____ Heroine   ____ Plot
   ____ Hero   ____ Inspirational theme
   ____ Setting   ____ Secondary characters

5. These characters were special because?_____

_____

_____

6. How has this book inspired your life?_____

_____

_____

7. What settings would you like to see covered in future
   Heartsong Presents books? _____

_____

_____

8. What are some inspirational themes you would like to see
   treated in future books? _____

_____

_____

9. Would you be interested in reading other **Heartsong
   Presents** titles? ❏ Yes ❏ No

10. Please check your age range:
    ❏ Under 18   ❏ 18-24
    ❏ 25-34   ❏ 35-45
    ❏ 46-55   ❏ Over 55

Name_____

Occupation _____

Address _____

City_____ State_____ Zip_____

ALABAMA

4 stories in 1

*N*estled in the northeastern mountains of Alabama is the fictional town of Rockdale. The small Southern town has become a haven for four women who have given up on finding love.

Four complete inspirational romance stories by author Kay Cornelius.

Contemporary, paperback, 480 pages, 5 ³/₁₆" x 8"

Heart♥ong

Presents